JUST A BITE

FUN-SIZED DRAGONS LOVE CURVES STORIES

AIDY AWARD

UNMASK ME

DRAGONS LOVE CURVES BOOK 2.5

ACKNOWLEDGMENTS

Thank you so much to the Amazeballs, my fabulous, amazing, reader group on Facebook. I've never giggled so much writing a book as I did you you all during our live writes.

Thanks for all your ideas that made this story even funnier and sexier than before and for your undying support. It means the world to me!

Special thanks to Carol Griggs Smith and Courtney Rehm for helping to last minute proofread this story. You all are the best.

Any remaining errors are totally my fault!

Extra hugs to Colorado Romance Writers and The Romance Chicks. This story would still be in the back of my head if it weren't for all of you. ;)

THE CHASE IS ON

*C*iara ran through the forest near the villa faster than her little feet had ever carried her before. She didn't run. Ugh. Stitch in her side already. Have to keep going. Why in the world did people do this for fun?

Normally she'd only run if zombies were chasing her. Or maybe if there was wine and cake at the finish line. Today held neither zombies nor cake. She was running from her mate, Jakob.

Ciara, my love. I'm going to get you.

From anyone else in her life, that would be creepy as all hell. Since it was the one man she loved above all others, who was also a big green dragon flying over the treetops, she wasn't scared even a little bit. She was actually having fun. Running. Who knew?

"Catch me if you can, you big green hunka-hunka burning love." Ciara dashed behind a really big tree that she knew had a knothole big enough for her to squeeze into, like a fairy cave. Jakob loved the chase. She'd discovered that when just running up or down the stairs turned him on. Since she'd discovered that adorable part of his dragon side, she'd taken advantage of it as often as possible.

Not like they needed an excuse to get each other dirty and naked. She was sure as heck getting dirty climbing into this hidey hole.

Milacku, a tree is not the best hiding place from me. That proud, tall, oak has already told me exactly where you are.

Ciara smacked the bark. "Traitor."

She crawled back out and didn't even make it to her feet before being tackled, ever so gently, by her giant green dragon. Jakob rolled with her, so that his scales were the only thing in the dirt, and he cradled his wings around her to protect her from any stray branches. In a blink of the eye, the green shimmering magic sparkled over his skin and he shifted into his human form.

His very naked human form. "Caught you."

The wind whipped around them both, and Ciara's light and flowy dress whipped up and over her head, hanging itself on a branch for later. "Goodie."

"I do love that you enjoy being caught as much as I enjoy catching you. Especially when you let me do this." Jakob waved a finger and some beautiful ivy vines crawled up the side of the tree. The leaves and vines tripled in size then wrapped themselves around her wrists like all-natural green handcuffs.

"You are a such a dirty dragon." Which she enjoyed immensely.

"I'm about to get dirtier." Jakob waggled his eyebrows at her and wound the vines around her waist and thighs. They tugged her legs open, so Ciara was spread wide and straddling him.

Oh my, this was going to be so good. Ciara wiggled her bum and strained against her leafy green bondage to get in the right position. She was already more than wet from the chase and the anticipation of the fun to come. Jakob would be able to slide his cock right in and she'd ride him like, well, a dragon.

Jakob had other plans. "Ah, ah, ah, naughty mate. You're not in charge right now and you don't get to dictate our fun. I'm going to have even more fun punishing you for that."

The vines holding her open for him lifted her slightly off the ground. Whoa. "Ack. I'm going to fall."

"Never." He scooted forward placing his hands on her inner thighs to help support the vines. "I'll never let you go and won't hurt you...except in the fun ways."

He emphasized his point by giving her a little bite to the spot between his hand and her pussy. A zing of lust shot through her and skittered across her skin shooting from her toes to her nose. That zing went haywire the moment his tongue tickled her clit.

Ciara groaned. If this was punishment, she was going to be naughty way more often. The more Jakob lapped at her sex, the more the ivy vines crept across her body, like shibari ropes, adding to the sensuality of her submission to everything he wanted to do to her. He played her body so expertly that within a few minutes she was already close to coming.

A vine wrapped around her throat, gently teasing her pulse, while more wrapped around her chest, shoulders, arms and head. "Yes, please, please, more, Jak--"

Her words were cut off when a leaf caressed her lips and her skin tingled with the tiniest burn. "Oh. Ohhhhh."

Jakob chuckled from beneath her legs. Why was he laughing? Dammit, he was giving her poison ivy. As soon as he gave her that orgasm that was milliseconds away, she was going to kill him.

The tingle she'd felt across her lips a moment ago spread across her body like wildfire. Like actual fire. Her skin burned, not enough to hurt, yet. Her crafty dragon with power of plants and earth knew exactly what he was doing. The burn prickled in every single erotic spot on her body. Behind her knee, the inside of her wrist, behind her ear, her lips, and her nipples were all glowing from the pleasure pain. The sear added a whole new element to the moment and pushed her body into overload, so many sensations that all seemed to stem from where Jakob's mouth lapped and suckled at her.

The orgasm built, spiraling all across her body, and she was so damn close that stars sparkled across her vision. "Don't stop. I'm gonna kill you later when I'm one big red welt, but don't stop. Please make me come, Jakob."

Her request didn't have her desired effect. Jakob pulled away leaving her panting on the verge of orgasm. "You forget you're being punished. You'll come when I tell you to."

The vines whipped her body around, and Jakob kneeled, positioning himself to take her from behind. He grabbed her hips and pushed his cock into her slick folds, sliding the head across her clit. "I can scent your need and it's intoxicating. I'll remember to play this game of pleasure and pain with you more often, love."

He cupped her breasts, swirling the poison ivy across her skin until the tingles turned to fire. She couldn't even get words out, her brain was fritzing. That's when Jakob thrust into her and pistoned his hips hard and fast. Every thrust sent her flying higher and higher.

"This is how I love to see you come, mindless for me and my cock, possessed by me and me alone." He reached around and with each thrust he swiped his fingers across her clit. "Come for me, *milacku*. Come for me now."

Ciara's body did exactly as she was told. With Jakob's command, her orgasm crashed down releasing all the tension that had coiled as tight as the vines around her body. She was already so consumed by the fiery bite of the poison ivy, Jakob's touch, and the intensity of his passion for her that all she could do was cry out his name and let the nirvana wash over them both.

Jakob groaned as her body clenched around him and he buried his face in her neck, scraping his teeth across the mark of the dragon he'd given her. His own release followed, and he pumped his seed deep into her.

Ciara never wanted this moment to end. She used her own magic to wrap them up in soft fluffy clouds of fog, secluding them in the forest in their own little bubble of love. It was peaceful and calm, but something niggled at the edge of her consciousness wanting to interrupt her warm glow.

A glow that was getting warmer by the second.

Warmer, and hotter, and scorching. Not in the fun way.

Holy poison ivy, Batman. "Jakob, Jakob, Jakob. Get me out of this stuff right this instant. I'm going to be so covered in red welts and a painful rash that you won't get to touch me for a month."

She squirmed to get away, but Jakob did nothing more than nuzzle her neck some more. "*Milacku*, I promised I would never hurt you, except in the fun ways. Did the burn of the poison ivy not intensify your pleasure? Your body and responses told me that you enjoyed every soft bite of pain."

"Shush your face. Of course I loved every second of it. But there isn't enough calamine lotion in the world to soothe the itching in places that should not itch." Ciara commanded the vines to retreat and examined her arms. Red splotches marred her skin up and down, backwards and forwards, inside and out.

Jakob kissed the mark of the green dragon in the curve between her neck and shoulder. A soft mist of Dragon's Breath floated across her skin, taking all the pain and redness away like magic. "Shall I breath my healing gift anywhere else?"

Uh. Duh. In her sexiest Poison Ivy the super villain voice she said, "Blow me, Jakob."

They spent the next half hour doing exactly that to each other until both Jakob and Ciara were satisfied all over again and she no longer had a single itch that needed to be scratched. They lay on soft grass and leaves together snuggling. The ivy leaves had retreated back to their normal shape and size around the base of the tree.

Ciara sat bolt upright staring at those leaves. The weather in the countryside has slowly gotten cooler over the past few weeks and soon all the leaves would likely be turning to the fabulous golds, reds, and oranges of fall. "What's the date?"

"It's the nineteenth of September."

Six weeks. Was that enough time to throw the Halloween party of the century? It would have to be.

Since she'd moved to the Czech Republic to be the mate of the Green Dragon Wyvern, she hadn't been bored for even a second. There was too much love making and fighting off demon dragons and finding more Green Dragons their fated mates. But she did miss the fun and anticipation of organizing a big party.

A Halloween party was no wedding, but that also meant she wouldn't have to deal with any Bridezillas. Plus, if she showed Jakob her hard-earned skills of her wedding planner trade maybe they could get their own wedding plans moving forward.

That is if he ever asked her to marry him for real. That Wyvern mating ceremony did not count, even if there had been a dress, a ring, and witnesses.

One thing at a time. "I think I'll go as Poison Ivy, the bad ass super villainess, to our Halloween party this year. Do you want to go as Batman or--?"

Jakob rolled over her and stared down into her eyes, all twinkly and distracting. "Are we having a Halloween party? That's not really a thing here."

"What do you mean it's not a thing?" Halloween was definitely a thing. Wasn't it invented in Europe in the first place?

"The Americans go a bit overboard, don't you think? Why don't we have a Christmas party instead, or maybe a little dinner party for Saint Mikuláš day?"

Oh, he wanted to see overboard? "Yes, let's have the dinner party and the Christmas party. You know we're doing American Thanksgiving in there too, and maybe for funsies, we'll do Canadian Thanksgiving, plus I'm sure we should have a fall harvest festival and a Black Friday fete, and maybe even a cyber Monday get together, oh, and I almost forgot about Boxing Day, and then it's New Years and we can have a huge bash for that."

Jakob's eyes got wider with each holiday she spouted out.

Then he narrowed his eyes and booped her on the nose. "I see you, Ciara. That shard of my soul you wear around your neck gives me access to all your hopes and fears. You can't bluster me. If you need a project to feel comfortable here in my home country like throwing a party, then do it. Throw the biggest party this country has ever seen."

Ciara threw her arms around his shoulders and peppered his face with kisses. "I knew there was a reason I loved you."

"I do love you and I want you to be happy." He ran a finger down her nose. "Just know that this will be an uphill battle."

"Battle schmattle. I've fought off a herd, or is it hoard, of demon dragons. I can conquer Europe's ignorance of how fun Halloween dress up parties are." For sure. No problem.

The whole walk back to the villa, Ciara made plans in her head. She couldn't wait to go to the city and shop for some party supplies. Jakob's home was sorely lacking all the basics of decorating. He had plenty of dragonalia, but not a single Christmas wreath, and definitely no pumpkins.

Oh no. Did they even have pumpkins in the Czech Republic? It wasn't Halloween without pumpkin carving. That would be the first thing she looked for in Prague. It was a major metropolitan city, surely they'd have everything she needed.

Jakob couldn't get away from Wyr business to go shopping with her in Prague, but he didn't want her to go on her own. Not with the continued demon dragon attacks. "I'm assigning Merc to be your bodyguard for the trip."

Merc, who was a mountain of a man so big that Ciara couldn't even imagine how huge his dragon form must be, stood outside next to a very nondescript blue Skoda sedan.

Jakob had a whole fleet of high-end fancy cars, but he insisted she take the teensy Skoda. The poop.

"Fine, but you know I can take care of myself." She rolled her eyes at him.

"Of course you can, love of my life, light of my soul, but I would die if anything happened to you. Placate me and be nice to Merc. He's not very good around women." Jakob looked a bit sly like he was planning something. "Don't tell him I said that."

Did Ciara smell some matchmaking plans from Jakob? Maybe she was rubbing off on him. "Okay, I'm off to shop till I drop. See you soon with tons of Halloween decorations, costumes, and candy. You should start thinking about what you want to dress up as."

Ciara gave him a quick kiss on the cheek, because anywhere else and her trip to Prague would be delayed by at least one dirty hour. She was already running late if she was going to get this bash put together and get the invites out in the next few weeks.

Too bad Jakob couldn't just fly her to Prague. It was okay, an hour in the car with the adorably awkward Merc would give her enough time to figure out the right kind of girl for him.

Merc held the door to the passenger side back seat open. No, no, no. He wasn't her chauffeur. They were going to be good friends by the end of the day. Ciara yanked the front door open and plopped into the seat, buckling herself in. Man, this car was so boring and plain. She supposed it was stealthier, but it needed some bling. Or at least a sparkly unicorn air freshener.

Lucky for Ciara, Merc was from the area and knew where

to take her for some shopping. She certainly didn't know where to find Halloween decorations, and while her Czech was coming along thanks to lessons from Jakob, the only useful phrases she knew how to say were hello and where's the bathroom. Everything else he'd taught her were only appropriate in the bedroom.

Merc probably wouldn't appreciate her asking him to spank her even if her pronunciation was perfect.

She spent the next hour grilling Merc with all sorts of questions on his personal preferences in women, but all she got was about fifty shades of him blushing and short one-word answers. He was going to be a tough case. He was probably more relieved when they pulled up to the first set of shops than she was excited.

"I'll park the car underground. It will be safest there." He drove them toward the car park, but Ciara shook her head.

"You're a dear. But I don't think I'm going to find the kind of Halloween supplies at IKEA." Yeah. He'd brought her to the Swedish superstore. Great for furnishing her college apartment maybe, not for throwing a party.

Merc's stomach growled and he blushed again.

"Oh, go on then. We'll have Swedish meatballs, lingonberry sauce, and some marzipan treats to start our afternoon off right. We'll need all our energy today, I think." She patted his arm. Whoa. He had more muscles than Jakob. Not that she was noticing. But some lucky girl was going to have so much fun being wrapped up in his arms.

Ciara was correct. They did need all their energy. Because after IKEA, where they did not find even one orange and black decoration, black cat, or even a bat wall hanging, Merc took her to about a dozen other shops.

Every single shop keeper looked at her like she was bonkers when Merc translated what she was looking for. None of them had a single pumpkin or jack-o-lantern. Not one.

She was close to tears when Merc parked the car near Malo Strana, the old part of town.

"Maybe we can find some costumes here." He sounded a bit desperate.

Not likely. Not after all the failures of the day. She followed him down the cobblestone streets and was ready to go get a beer and some fried cheese from one of the street vendors when she spied the cutest little shop that had a window full of classic witch hats, brooms, and even a black cat in the window.

Yes. Finally. She gave Merc a shove toward the shop. "There, let's try that place."

He held the door open for her and a tingle-lingle-ling sounded as she walked into the sweet-smelling floor room.

"Hello, welcome to Inanna's Emporium for Witches and other Goddesses. How can I help you today?"

DRAGONS DON'T WEAR COSTUMES

One phone call down, about a million more to go. Ky thought a Halloween party would be fun, so he was coming over from New Zealand for it. That's why Jakob called the Blue Wyvern first. Cage, the Gold Wyvern thought it sounded like fun too and would fly down from Denmark. Ky and Cage were easy peasy. They would be here with bells on and any other costumes Ciara required of them. Both of them adored Ciara and would do anything to make her feel welcome.

Match was another story.

As the alpha of alphas, his approval was more important than Jakob wanted to admit. As the Red Wyvern, Match acknowledged Ciara, he fought to keep her safe as a Wyvern's mate was precious, but he was still reticent about a human, especially one who had powers like Ciara. Grumpy bastard.

If the love of his life hadn't insisted that he call each and every Wyvern and get them to come to her party, Jakob would purposefully leave Match to his cold lair in Poland. What the hell a fire dragon did in the frigid winters was beyond Jakob.

Prague had its fair share of snow, but as a Green Dragon he understood the value of rest and renewal before the spring.

It was like Match was torturing himself.

Jakob dialed Match's number. Then he hung up. There was one more dragon he could call first. If Ciara was determined to celebrate like the Americans, he would bring her reinforcements.

Steele picked up the phone after one ring. "Hey, boss. No new demon dragons here in New York to report."

"Good. I imagine the wolves have them on the run." Steele had done a great job laying inroads for the Green Dragons in America. Jakob couldn't have chosen better for his second in command. "But that's not why I'm calling. What do you know about Halloween?"

"Uh." That meant he knew as much as any dragon. Nothing. "It's the day after All Hallows Eve?"

Well, at least Jakob wasn't the only dumbass. "I think that's the same thing."

"Fleur has the kids from her school garden project growing big orange squashes because she says they're going to carve them for Halloween. I don't know what happens after that, but it has something to do with the party they throw."

Aha. Fleur was mostly American and a little bit Greek flower nymph. She was the perfect mate for Steele and would be the perfect helper for Ciara. "Fleur needs to come to the Green Dragon homeland and help my mate with her party. Put her on the phone, please."

Jakob heard some kissing and soft-spoken words before a woman's voice came through the phone. "This is Fleur, at your service, my liege."

She giggled, teasing Jakob with the honorific title. He liked

Steele's mate. Her smart mouth suited a Green Dragon Warrior perfectly. "Can you please explain my mate's fascination with Halloween and why she needs to cut up orange squashes?"

Fleur squealed at a very high pitch. "I love Halloween. We're growing pumpkins to carve into Jack-o-lanterns at school. But where is Ciara going to get them over there? They are native to the Americas."

Seemed like a waste of squash. Wouldn't it be better roasted with pork, or maybe duck? He'd have to get his cook to make that for dinner. "What is a Jack-O-Lantern and where can I get, say a hundred of them for her party?"

More squealing from Fleur floated through the line. She was an excitable woman just like his Ciara. They would be good company for each other. He should have thought to have Steele and Fleur back to the villa more often.

"She's having a party? A dress up one? Steele, can you fly us over to Prague and back in time for the kids costume parade?"

"I have already requested your presence to help Ciara, if you don't mind. I'm afraid she is going to run into more obstacles than she realizes."

"Sweet. I'll see if Heli or Galyna can fill in at the children's parade and we'll come over a few days early. I can bring seeds. We'll have the whole front garden turned into a pumpkin patch overnight."

Good thing he lived out in the country. The nearby village was about to get one heck of a new fall harvest farmer's market. "Thank you, Fleur. I look forward to having you and Steele here."

That call eased his mind enough that he was thinking much more clearly. He wasn't going to simply call Match and invite him. That would get him an earful about how a party wasn't a Wyvern's responsibility and how they should all be on the hunt for the mysterious Black Dragon. Yes, they needed to keep humankind safe from the machinations of hell. But the Dragon Warriors worked hard training, fighting, and defending all that was good and right in the world from the demon wyrms. They deserved a chance at the same happiness Jakob had.

Even fucking Match.

Ciara's party was just the thing Dragonkind needed right now.

He dialed up Ky and Cage again, enlisting their help for his plan. Then he conferenced in Match.

"What do you want, Green?" Same old grumpy ass Red Dragon.

"Bro, calm your tatas. Jakob has new intel. Listen up." Ky was never bothered by Match's dark moods.

Cage covered a laugh with a cough. "Yes, brother. This is important. You're going to want in on this."

"Fine. What?" They could practically hear him roll his eyes.

Jakob could imagine the smoke rolling out of Match's nostrils. If anyone in the world needed a mate to soothe the beast within, it was the Red Dragons. They were all so intense in their deep hatred of the demon dragons, the Wyvern most of all.

"I've learned of an upcoming, um, outbreak of monsters planned for the end of October on my villa. It presents the perfect opportunity for us to do some undercover surveillance." Yeah, that was clear as mud. Hopefully Match wouldn't hear anything but monsters.

Match growled. "What are you on about? An outbreak of monsters? Does this have something to do with your mate?"

"Inevitably." Ky replied with more than a hint of humor in his voice.

Match harrumphed. "She is a trouble magnet."

One that Jakob was sure all of his dragon brothers was jealous of. Sometimes he was jealous of himself for being so lucky to have such an amazing gift like Ciara in his life.

"And each and every one of us pray for a woman just like her for our own," Cage slipped in reflecting Jakob's thoughts. Sometimes it was like Cage had super secret sneaky spy tech that could look right inside everyone's thoughts.

"Hmph," was all Match could reply. Because they all knew Cage was right.

Maybe Ciara could use her wedding planner skills and find mates for more dragons at her party. "I need you all to fly down here on the last day of the month and participate in the foray."

"Your American has made you speak strangely. I will be there. Now leave me be. I have demons of my own to search out." Match hung up.

Ky and Cage stayed on the line. "That went better than I expected. He likes her, you know."

He sure had a funny way of showing it. "If you say so. He's going to kill us when he finds out he's been roped into a fancy-dress party."

"Which makes it even more fun." Cage was always up for a good prank. "Does Ciara have direction on what kind of costumes she wants us in? I think we should go as a boy band."

Ky sighed. "Just because you're obsessed with Lars Ulrich, does not mean we're going as Metallica."

"Come on. You know you want to." Cage could talk a polar bear into buying ice to bring to the party. Jakob had no doubt that he'd talk Ky and Match into some kind of ridiculous get ups that would please Ciara enormously.

"No way. If we're going as a band, it's got to be the Dragons. Duh." Ky was very proud of all things New Zealand.

Actually, if there was really a Kiwi band called the Dragons, they really should go as them. But would anyone besides Ky even know who they were? Jakob wanted everything to be perfect for Ciara. "I'm leaving the costumes up to you two. If you can even get Match to show up in a mask it will be a coup worthy of a toast with Dragon's Breath infused wine. I'll bring out my oldest vintage and have it waiting."

"You're on." Cage always loved a good bet.

Ciara's voice floated into the office. "Jakob. I'm home and I'm making a banana split. You want one?"

Uh-oh. Ice cream was high on Ciara's comfort foods list. Dammit. He knew the shopping trip to Prague wouldn't go how she wanted.

"You two hash out the costumes. I've got to go take care of my mate." Jakob hung up on the other Wyverns and put boy band costumes into the back of his mind.

He found Ciara in the kitchen already piling on long squirts of whipped cream from a can. That shouldn't even be a thing, but he could think of a few things to do with whipped cream that did not include an ice cream sundae but did have him licking all of her sweetness. "*Milacku*, come here and tell me what's wrong."

"Nothing you can fix, unless you've got hoard of

Halloween decorations down in your lair." She slumped onto a stool at the kitchen counter and scooped up a big bite of her ice cream. "I know I can pull off this party, but I don't want your dragons to think I'm a flibberty-gibbet who can't do anything right."

"Love, I don't know what a flibberty-gibbet is, but I doubt you are one. Unless it means sexiest mate ever to be found. Then you definitely are that." He wrapped his arms around Ciara and swiped his finger into the creamy topping. He brought his finger up to her luscious mouth and painted her lips with the sweet treat.

Ciara made mean eyes at his finger, but then gave in and licked just the tip. That wouldn't do. "More than the tip, Ciara. Take more."

"Your mind is eternally in the gutter, isn't it?" The crankiness was slowly leaving her voice and those sultry tones he loved were coming back.

"My mind is well below the gutter when it comes to you sucking any part of my body, love." Jakob pushed his fingers into her mouth and Ciara swirled her tongue around and around, sucking off every single bit of the cream there.

"Are you sure we have to throw this party? I would be perfectly happy to celebrate the holiday with just the two of us playing dress up...in bed."

She bit the end of his finger then smiled so innocently when he jerked it away. "Jakey-poo. You're very good at distracting me with your dirty talk, but yes, we are having this Halloween party. I want all of the dragons in your Wyr to come and have fun."

"I simply hate to see you upset over the Europe-wide lack of Halloween decorations." He swiped his finger into the whipped cream again and this time wanting to avoid her cranky bite, dribbled it over her neck and collarbone, right over the green dragon mark he'd given her.

He lowered his head and scraped his teeth across her skin and soothed the bite with his tongue. Ciara pushed her hands into his hair and tipped her head to the side to give him more access. "I guess we could have that Thanksgiving celebration instead, but I think that will be even harder since only Americans and Canadians celebrate that particular holiday."

Ooh. A drip of the ice cream snaked a path from her mark and toward her ample cleavage. He wasn't stopping that bit of dessert from its journey until it reached the final destination. Then he'd follow it with his tongue. Hmm. He would probably have to remove her shirt and bra to get to ever last bit of cream.

"Jakob, are you even paying attention?" She sighed.

Busted. "Of course I am. I'm paying very close attention to how I can make you very, very happy in the next few minutes."

"Mmm-hmm. What do you think I should do then?"

Uh-oh. Had she asked him a question. He'd better think fast, or she'd get mad and then no one was going to be happy tonight. "I'm not sure, but what if we altered your party just a little and instead of a Halloween party, we made it a masquerade ball? My Wyr will understand that idea better and you can decorate however you'd like."

The dribble of ice cream disappeared for good and in about three seconds this conversation was going to be over, because he was going to have her up on the counter, naked, licking her from head to toe and back again.

"A masquerade? Oh, and also... can you please do that thing

with your tongue right here?" She pointed to the divot between her breasts.

How the hell was she able to continue this conversation and party plan at the same time? That was talent. "Yes, it's the perfect way for our Green Dragon Wyr to let loose and I bet if you invited every woman between here and Paris, more than a few of them will find their mates."

Ciara gasped and then froze. "Find their mates?"

Jakob carefully nodded his head. "Yes. I believe now that Steele has found Fleur, the curse on the Green Dragons is over and they can all be as lucky as I am."

Ciara grasped Jakob's head and kissed him hard on the lips. But it was over so fast, he didn't even get a chance to slip her some tongue. "You are a genius, dragon. A masquerade ball with full on costumes and masks where everyone finds love is my jam. Merc is going to look perfect dressed up as a knight in shining armor. No woman will be able to resist. He is at the top of my find a mate list."

She hopped off the stool and headed toward the back door where the cars were parked. "I even stopped in a very fancy costume emporium. The woman who ran it talked me into buying a bunch of stuff that seemed a bit over the top for a Halloween party, but will be perfect for a fancy-dress masquerade ball

Shit. He'd only said what he thought she wanted to hear so he could get her naked and moaning his name sooner. Where was she going if it wasn't up to their bedroom? He'd just have to get bossy with her, because they both liked it when he did. "Ciara Mosely-Willingham, you get your pretty ass back here right now."

Ciara stopped and pivoted with her hands on her hips. She

raised an eyebrow at him and made the mean face, but her eyes had that lusty twinkle in them. "You'd better have a good reason for stopping me when I'm on a roll, buster."

Jakob had a lot of very hard reasons. Namely in his pants. "You've got ice cream down your shirt. You don't want to get those fancy costumes all messy, do you?"

She thought for a moment. "No. I don't."

"Then come over here and let me clean you up." He quirked a finger at her.

She tried very hard to suppress her grin, but she did walk back over and right in between his legs. "Why do I think that means we're about to get very, very dirty?"

"Because it does. Besides, you walked away with my snack down your shirt." As soon as she looked down, he popped the top two buttons of her shirt open and dove in headfirst.

PUMPKIN-PALOOZA

*O*nly one week from the masquerade ball and hundreds of dragons from all of the Wyrs were coming. Even more people from the surrounding villages were pee-in-their pants excited to be invited to the mysterious villa in the Czech countryside. Only a select few humans knew the true nature of Jakob Zeleny and his dragons, so it was a pretty big deal that he was hosting a party for any and all who wanted to join in the Halloween merry making.

In fact, the guest list had grown so large that the party was going to have to be held mostly outdoors. Ciara had bribed Cage Gylden, the too flirty Gold Dragon Wyvern, to help her bring in some warm southern winds to keep the evening snow-storm free. All it had cost her was a dance... which she would have to find a way to distract Jakob during. Her lovely, hunky mate had a bit of a green jealous streak.

Not that she minded one bit. She loved knowing her man wanted her enough to be jealous in the first place. She hadn't always thought she'd have someone in her life that loved her like that, and she thanked her lucky stars and the White Witch for bringing them together.

Jakob rounded the corner into the garden where Ciara was working her magic hard to grow a living structure that she wanted to hang fairy lights all around. He had a huge box of squash and turnips that no mere mortal should be able to even lift, much less carry around like it weighed nothing more than cotton candy.

"Where do you want these?"

Ciara pointed to a long wooden picnic table. "There, at our pumpkin carving station."

"But these aren't pumpkins."

She was still throwing a masquerade ball, but with a Halloween theme. No Halloween party was complete without pumpkin carving. Jakob had nixed the apple bobbing citing that the guests would not like to get their masks wet. Everyone would be going home with a bag of the good trick or treating candy. Lots of Reese's peanut butter cups and no gross generic orange and black wrapped taffy-toffee disgusting blobs of candy. "I know. I'm making do."

"You're making something spectacular, love. I doubt there has ever been a party the likes of ours in all of Czech history." He kissed her on the top of the head and unloaded the vegetables.

Something important had been on Ciara's mind about that exact thing. "You know, if this is a way for lots of our green dragons to find mates, we should invite more than all the pretty Czech girls from the area. You had to go all the way to America to find me. What if none of their soul shards light up. Everyone will be so disappointed. The party would be a complete failure."

Never once in her long and storied career as a wedding planner had she ever failed. Even the worst of bridezillas or mother of the bridezillas could be calmed, lovers' quarrels could be solved, and even amorous drunken groomsmen could be distracted so disasters were diverted. But this wasn't a wedding and there would be more couples than she could keep an eye on. What if none of them turned out to be mates?

Ciara felt a little sick to her stomach. Having a party like this flopping was the stuff of nightmares for a planner such as herself. She would be so embarrassed if everyone came and no one found a mate.

"I doubt that will happen, love. We've been getting more reports everyday of our greens finding mates. With so many of them gathered together, the odds are in our favor."

She looked up at the sky and pressed her hands together. "I just need a little matchmaking spell, please."

Jakob looked up and then narrowed his eyes at her. "You haven't been conspiring with the White Witch again, have you? Your power over the elements has been coming along just fine without her interference."

She hadn't seen Mrs. Bohacek or any other magical woman for a while. But it was fun to keep Jakob on his toes. "That would be something wouldn't it? But no. I wouldn't mind some help to make sure everything goes great with this shindig."

"Would it help if I told you I invited Steele, Fleur, and Wesley to come over for your party?" Jakob asked his question all nonchalantly, but he peeked at her waiting to see what she'd do. The sneak.

She didn't let him down one bit. Ciara leaped across the two feet of lawn and climbed him like a tree, peppering him with kisses all the way up. "You are the best dragon mate a girl could ever have. Why didn't you tell me sooner, you sexy butt-head?"

"Simply so I could get a reaction like this." Jakob grabbed her thighs and wrapped them around his waist then set her rear-end on the edge of the table and ground their naughty bits together.

They spent more time than she'd planned in her schedule making out. And yes, she had penciled in time for kissy face with her favorite dragon because it would be dumb not too since it would one hundred percent be happening every day. Sadly, Ciara put a stop to their hanky panky before he got his hands on her panties.

If their friends from America were coming, she needed to redouble her efforts to make this party spectacular and that would cut into sexy times. Well, at least until later when it was marked down on the minute by minute planner.

She tried to wiggle away but didn't get far. Jakob's kisses were just too delicious. She stuck a hand in between Jakob's lips and hers, but he licked her fingers one by one making very lewd motions with his tongue. "Stop that or I won't get any work done. When do they arrive?"

"Who?" Jakob shoved a hand between her thighs. He wasn't quite ready to give up on those panties.

Ciara smacked his hand away from underneath her skirt. "Steele, Fleur, and Wesley."

"Ahem." Someone cleared his throat nearby. "We can come back later, boss, if this is a bad time."

Jakob pressed his forehead to Ciara's and sighed. "Surprise. They're here. Several hours early by the way."

Ciara turned and saw Steele, the Green Wyr's second in

command and his mate Fleur walking into the back garden. She jumped up to run and greet them, paused for a second and blew Jakob a kiss. "Stick that in your pants and save it for later."

Then she ran and enveloped Fleur in a giant hug. "I'm so glad you're here. I've been dying to talk to anyone else on the planet who understands the amazingness of Halloween."

They squealed together for an appropriate amount of time and then Ciara dragged Fleur over to the living structure she'd been making. "You're so much better with the Earth element than I am, would you mind fluffing up the leaves here just in case it rains?"

Without even a thought, Fleur waved her fingers and the flagging plants on Ciara's shelter turned into a gorgeous gazebo complete with flowers and fruit dangling from the vines. "How's that?"

"Fabulous. I have got to practice my Earth magic with you while you're here."

"I brought you a present." Fleur grinned and held a tiny burlap bag tied with a ribbon out to her. "Open it, open it."

Ciara slipped the ribbon off and tipped the bag, so the content fell into her hand. "Pumpkin seeds. Yes, yes, yes. You are fricking brilliant. I had no idea where I was going to get pumpkins."

The two of them rushed over to an empty-ish plot in the yard and scattered the seeds on the ground. "This is a good chance to practice growing things. I know Jakob loves it when I do."

Fleur held their hands over the little seeds and a shimmering green magic drifted over the ground. The pumpkins were scone-sized in seconds. "Oh, yes. Nothing gets Steele turned on faster than dirt and greenery. I should have stock in the local mineral hot springs for how often we go to their mud baths."

"Oh my gawd, I have to get one of those. Maybe Ky Puru will help me find a water source. Although, after the party, I'll never get anything done if Jakob even gets a whiff of a mud bath for us."

"Are all the Wyverns coming? Ky and Cage are cool, but that Match. Whew." Fleur adjusted Ciara's hand to help a flagging little pumpkin get some magic too. It ballooned up to the size of a big dog in no time.

"Oops. Too much. Oh, well, we can use that one for a cooler. The Czech beer here is amazing." They chose a couple that were just the right size for carving. "Match is okay. Jakob say he just needs to get laid. It'll take a strong woman to tame that beast."

Merc rounded the corner into the back garden with another load of the squash and stopped short at the pumpkins growing in front of the girls. "What are those things?"

Ciara giggled. Green Dragons were suckers for learning about new plants. Merc had that curiosity sparkle to his eye like a little kid who'd just discovered puppies. "Pumpkins."

"What are they for, more decorations?" He set his box down and circled the little pumpkin patch, kneeling and examining each gourd.

"We're going to carve them. It's fun, you'll see."

"That seems like a strange thing to do." He picked up one pumpkin that had fallen on its side and grew into an oblong shape.

Ciara elbowed Fleur. "See, I told you they don't get it."

Fleur nodded sagely. "I guess we'll just have to show them."

"Absolutely. Come on, Merc. Your pumpkin carving skills are going to impress all the women at the party tomorrow."

"Uh." Merc held up a finger as if to say something to stop the festivities.

Ciara and Fleur grabbed him by the arms and drug him and his pumpkin over to the table. They set their own choices down and Ciara prepared to demonstrate the fine art of jack-o-lanterning. "Wait, we don't have knives and scoopers. How are we going to hollow them out and make faces?"

"I got this," Steele said. He shifted one talon and cut the top of the pumpkin right off.

"You're so hot when you use your claws all domestically like that." Fleur made bedroom eyes at him and a little daisy popped up in Steele's hair.

Not to be outdone, Jakob chopped up a pumpkin and scooped the seeds and guts out. "Okay now what do we do with this mess? It would be very creepy as a costume. You could fulfill your strange American fascination with zombies and wear them as undead guts."

Ciara snorted. "No babe. The pumpkin seeds are delicious baked and salted. We're going to carve the pumpkins and put candles inside to make decorations."

Merc picked up his oblong squash and turned it over in his hands. "Like vegetable artwork?"

"Yes. Exactly, you got it." She patted them on the back and in a moment of inspiration challenged them to a competition. "Let's see what you boys come up with, while Fleur and I grow some more pumpkins for our guests. Winner gets a kiss."

The guys went to work and wouldn't let her and Fleur see their creations until they were done. It gave them plenty of time to grow a whole hoard of pumpkins for the festivities.

She and Jakob were going to be eating pumpkin pie, pumpkin cookies, pumpkin bread, pumpkin muffins, and pumpkin spiced lattes for like a thousand years.

"Are you three done with your masterpieces yet?" Ciara tried to peek over their shoulders, but Jakob kept blocking her.

He set his pumpkin down on the table with a flourish and stepped aside, waving Vanna White style to his jack-o-lantern. "Yes. Now you must judge the winner, *milacku,* and give me your prize."

Uh-oh. Jakob's competitive side was out to play. The other two guys moved to the side revealing quite a mess of pumpkin guts and artistry. They should all be on the Food Network with these skills. This was Pumpkin Wars, Dragon edition at its finest.

Ciara raised an eyebrow at Jakob. "Have you been secretly practicing?"

He folded his arms and looked back at her all smug and sexy-like. "No. Green Dragons have superior skills when it comes to vegetable artistry."

Steele and Jakob had each carved elaborate scenes of dragons. Jakob's was a scene with a big dragon squashing demon wyrms, which was very impressive. Steele's showed a dragon peeking out from behind a forest of trees and a full moon high in the sky. There was even a pack of wolves howling up at the moon.

Then there was Merc's creation. He hadn't hollowed his squash out but had intricately carved a very life-like... penis. Like it had veins and ridges, and - oh god, was that a pile of pumpkin seeds coming out of the tip? She should have known. Boys.

She exchanged a look with Fleur and before their dragons could protest, they both gave Merc a kiss on his cheeks. "Merc wins."

He turned about forty-two shades of pink, but also looked very pleased with himself. Jakob and Steele took their loss graciously. Probably because both knew they would get their rewards later.

Jakob definitely got his prize that night. Twice.

The day of the party dawned and still Wes hadn't shown up. Ciara knew full-well it would be a miracle for him to get away from Willingham Weddings on a big holiday like this. There were way more goth weddings than anyone knew, and they all had to be held on Halloween, so she doubted he would even make it. Too bad. She missed him and he always had such great costumes.

No time to think about that today. She had a million and seven things to do before everyone arrived. After coffee. While Jakob snored away, Ciara snuck out of bed and down to the kitchen to start a caffeine IV drip. As she got closer and closer, she was sure she already smelled the coffee brewing.

"Hello, Ciara dear. Cream and sugar for you?" A steaming mug was already poured for her and the little pot of cream and the bowl of sugar floated over to her regular seat at the kitchen island.

Ciara plonked down on the stool and waited while the cream poured itself and the sugar spoon gave the whole drink a stir. "Mrs. Bohacek? What are you doing here?"

"Just fiddling with your guest list, a bit. You missed a few people you wanted to invite." Mrs. Bohacek was scribbling away in one of the planners Ciara had been using for the masquerade ball.

She didn't get a chance to protest that particular invasion because she was hit with a vision and was trying not to hurl in her coffee. She had a feeling she was going to need all the energy she could get. In her mind's eye the party she'd planned down to the most minute detail played like a movie. Green Dragons' soul shards were gleaming all around the room as they mingled, signaling that they were about to find their mates. But for some reason she couldn't see any of the mates.

A beautiful woman in a white flowing toga floated across the room looking worried. With her was a man with a prosthetic arm who looked like a hotter version of Jason Momoa, dressed up as Julius Caesar but his laurel wreath headband was rainbow colored leaves. He pointed directly at Ciara. In a creepy haunted kind of voice he said, "Beware the Ides of... no wait, that's not right. Beware of looking a gift demon in the mouth. No, that's not it either, although it's still good advice. Let me think."

The woman in the white toga rolled her eyes. "The incubus, dear heart."

"Right. Got it. Beware of Greek sex-demons bearing gifts." The man frowned and pulled the woman to him, kissing her on the hand. "Isn't that a little cryptic, my love? He's not Greek, he's Sumerian, and we don't even know if he and his Galla Demons are going to be here."

"Better safe than sorry, and I think our white witch-in-training gets the gist." The woman looked at Ciara and patted her cheek. "Good luck at your party, Ciara."

Ciara blinked and it took a minute to get her bearings. She had to grab onto the chair to keep from toppling over. Only, it wasn't the kitchen chair in her grasp, it was one of the

outdoor folding chairs she'd had brought in for the party. She
wasn't even in the kitchen. She was in the back yard and the
sun wasn't rising, it was setting.

Was this still a vision? She pinched herself to make sure.
"Ouch."

"Ciara, my love. What's wrong?" Jakob wrapped an arm
around her. He was dressed in his costume for the night and
his brilliant green eyes sparkled down at her through his
mask.

Ciara touched her own face and found her mask was on
too. Crapballs. She'd lost the whole day to that vision, which
was already fading from her memory with each second. At
least the White Witch had helped her skip all the pre-party
stress. "Nothing. Nothing at all. We should probably greet our
guests. "

Lots of dragons from all the Wyrs had shown up. There
were about a dozen Thors, a group who'd come dressed as the
Beatles, another as the Addams Family, and she spotted Merc
dressed as a very sexy Zorro.

"Wait. What did you and the other Wyverns come as?"

"If he figures it out, he's going to kill us. I don't even know
how Cage and Ky talked me into it." Jakob took a step back
and slowly spun for her.

"Oh my God. He is going to murder you in the face with
his dragon's fire. He hasn't seen you yet?" Ciara had to cover
her mouth to keep from guffawing.

"No, and I think I see him coming this way. Don't tell
anyone that I'm hiding in the beer garden."

"Go, hurry. I'll run interference." She shooed her very
brave mate away and searched the crowd for Match. Jakob

was being paranoid. She did spy someone else she was excited to see though.

"Wesley?" She waved and pushed through the crowd. "Is that you?"

He sauntered toward her like he didn't have a care in the world. The crowd parted for him and as soon as he reached her, Wes spun her to look at her whole costume. "Darling, you look stunning as always. The Maid Marion look is a good one for you. Here, this gift is for you."

He handed her a glass of champagne.

She'd chosen to go as the heroine from the Robin Hood tale mostly because she got to wear the dark green velvet dress she'd worn on the day she'd mated Jakob. She hugged Wesley and had to ward off a chill in the air. "You made it. How in the world did you get my mother to give you Halloween off? Isn't that big goth wedding today?"

"Your mother never could resist my charms." He waggled his eyebrows at her.

"Ew. Don't be disgusting." She looked at his costume and mask which was not exactly his normal style. She expected drag queen. but she'd call this more, uh, au natural. "Who are you dressed as?"

His eyes twinkled with humor through the slots of the mask decorated very elegantly with some kind of fruit motif. Was that a pomegranate?

He glanced around the room like he was about to tell her a secret. "You know the story of Persephone and how her descent into Hell marks the seasons' change?"

"Yeah, but you're no Persephone." That was a Greek myth, right?

He laughed kind of weirdly. "No. The myth comes from an older Sumerian story of a brother who saves his lovely sister from a punishment in hell by sacrificing himself. They each must spend half the year in hell, meeting only on the equinoxes of each year, thus bringing forth spring and winter."

"Seriously? You're this, uh, brother from hell?" Wes was weird sometimes. He knew the strangest crap.

He looked her straight in the eye and without even a hint of humor he said, "Yes, I'm Dumuzid."

Okay then. "Where is your sister? Did you bring a date? Do I get to meet him?"

"Geshtianna is in hell," he deadpanned. "But I would never come to your masquerade empty handed, witchikins. I brought just the girl for one very special dragon."

"Oh." Ciara clapped. "I've got just the one. He's a little bit shy, but very sweet and I'd love to find him a girlfriend."

Wes turned back to her to say something and caught her examining Merc in his Zorro costume. "Your gaydar is off as always, sweets. That man is looking for a sword, not a... whatever, insert hilarious vagina joke here. For being able to get a glimpse of the dragons' mates in advance, you are a horrible matchmaker."

"And now I've got -Matchmaker, matchmaker make me a match- stuck in my head." Also... when had she told Wes about her mates' visions?

"Don't quit your day job, honey." He wrinkled his nose at her singing. "Now introduce me to these Wyverns you talk so much about."

"You've met them all. There are only four. Match isn't here yet." She indicated toward the beer garden area where Jakob, Ky, and Cage were chatting.

"Oh. Right. Of course. Then I'm off to mingle. Maybe I can hook my date up with one of them." He waved at a woman with curves for miles dressed in black leather like a plus sized biker Barbie who gave off a serious sex-on-a-stick vibe. "Portia, let's find you your dragon, sweetheart."

Wes moved into the crowd and toward biker Barbie and took her by the elbow leading her toward a group of dragons that had intercepted and surrounded Cage, the Gold Wyvern. Weird that Wes had brought a girl with him. She couldn't blame him for making friends or anything and since she'd moved to Europe they certainly didn't get to hang out or even talk as much as they used to.

Maybe Wes was a bit resentful of her new life living with a dragon shifter mate. He sure seemed... different tonight. Well, poop. But no time to worry about him now. She had some matchmaking of her own to do. Now, where was Merc?

AMUCK, AMUCK, AMUCK

*C*iara's Halloween masquerade ball was in full swing and while everything looked like it was going great on the surface, something was amiss. Jakob just couldn't quite put his finger on it.

He was sipping on a fine Czech Pilsner in the beer garden section of the party surveying the guests. Cage had gone off with a pretty woman in leather, which was totally his type. Too bad she hadn't lit up his soul shard. It would be nice if Jakob wasn't the only Wyvern with a mate. He knew that sometimes Ciara got a little lonely and wished for other dragon mates to talk to. Hopefully many of his Green Dragon Warriors would find mates tonight.

Hmm. So far, not so much.

Ky Puru, the Blue Wyvern from New Zealand grabbed a bottle from the pumpkin cooler and clinked it against Jakob's. "Hey Bro. You haven't seen Match, yet, huh?"

"I think you'd know if I had. You'd better have your ice ready to put out our clothes when he shoots flames at our asses for dressing up as a grumpy version of him."

Ky tapped his cheek and frozen mist floated out of his nose. "Ready and waiting. He could shoot lava and it would still be worth it."

Jakob pointed to a couple who thought they were hidden among the bushes making out but were pretty much making out right in front of the whole party. They couldn't get enough of each other, just like Jakob couldn't get enough of Ciara. He jerked his chin toward the couple. "Is it weird that so many dragon warriors are hooking up with women they are very into, but none of them have found a true mate?"

Ky raised an eyebrow. "Dude. You know dragon warriors are horny as. Besides, you can't expect everyone to find mates just because you and a few others of your Greens have. It's still a rare occurrence.

"It just seems suspicious that with such a large gathering of dragons, not a single soul shard has lit up." Jakob took a swig of his pilsner and looked for Ciara. He hoped she hadn't noticed yet. It was really going to bum her out if no one found a mate tonight.

She'd had a weird day as it was, sort of in a fog. He'd put it off as her being stressed about last minute details, but that wasn't her usual M. O.

His gut instincts to defend and protect her were raging and he could not figure out why. It was a fucking party, people were having fun, but Dragons weren't finding mates.

Every cell of his being screamed at him to do something other than stand around dressed as a grumpy red dragon. Ciara would kill him if he whisked her away from the party simply for being paranoid. Besides the fact that if he ruined her party, she'd never let him in her pants ever again.

If he ever needed to figure out how to be a Wyvern, it was

now. His own needs never came before that of his Wyr. Match would kick his ass if he ever even thought that Jakob had been thinking with his dick when there could be a potential threat.

A guest that Jakob didn't recognize by sight or scent approached him with an outstretched hand looking for a beer. Jakob grabbed one and popped the lid off with a quick change of his talon. He offered it to Julius Caesar with the rainbow crown. He lifted his own beer in toast. "*Na zdravi.*"

Caesar tipped his beer toward Jakob in a thank-you gesture. "*Na zdravi.* You green dragons always were good hosts. This is one heck of a party."

"There is something amiss." Wait. Why did he say that? He should not be getting anyone else worried, especially not a guest he didn't know.

"Why do you say that?" The dragon took a sip of the beer and looked around the party. "I don't see anything."

What he meant to say was - Never mind. That was better than putting this warrior on alert for no reason. But what came out of his mouth was, "It's a gut feeling."

The other warrior nodded. "Hmm. I tend to trust those. Got me my mate after all."

Jakob knew every one of his green dragon warriors. This was not one of them. That meant there was a dragon from another Wyr with a mate. Couldn't be. His skin tingled as the hairs on the back of his neck stood up. It appeared this was a new clue in the case of not-everything-is-as-it-appears.

He doubted outright asking the warrior who he was would work. No Jakob needed to be much stealthier than that. "The other Wyverns are all having a lot of fun. No need to worry them or anyone else."

Ky was showing off some tricks with water and ice to a

group of giggling woman and Cage - huh. Cage had disappeared. Probably off romancing some pretty starry-eyed gold-digger. Match still wasn't even here yet.

Caesar finished his beer and grabbed another. "You are the youngest Wyvern in a long time, my boy. Barely in your Prime. I can see why you think Maciej Cervony's opinion matters so much."

What the hell? Jakob hadn't said a thing about Match or being a young Wyvern. "Now, just a minute."

The warrior put a hand on Jakob's shoulder and a surge of power flowed through him like the first time he'd met Ciara. It rumbled through his veins and made him feel invincible. The dragon looked him straight in the eye. "You're the one who broke the spell over our people that has lasted almost seven hundred years, Jakob Zeleny. You, the Green Dragon Wyvern. You found your mate when no other had and changed the tide of our war against the dark forces of hell."

Jakob swallowed fighting back the urge to shift into his dragon form immediately. "The White Witch and the First Dragon blessed me with Ciara. I didn't do anything."

"No? You didn't cross an ocean three times, battle a thousand Galla demons, get a powerful witch to fall in love with you, then fight a thousand more Galla demons, sacrificing your own soul to keep her safe?"

Oh, well, yeah. He had done all of that. "I did."

The dragon raised an eyebrow and his crown sparkled with magic and power. "Has the Gold, Blue, Red, or any other Wyvern done any of that and broken the spell on their own Wyrs?"

"No. But the White Witch and the First Dragon haven't--" Jakob didn't finish that sentence because even to his own ears he was making excuses, making himself into an imposter. No one knew what the White Witch and the First Dragon did from the afterlife. Maybe the two of them were playing matchmaker and no one else had figured it out. "Who are you, venerable warrior?"

Caesar grinned and more power surged into Jakob. "Just someone sent to tell you to get your head out of your butt and trust your instincts. You don't need any grumpy red dragons to tell you who you are and what you can do. Just fucking do it, kid."

Jakob searched his heart and felt the warrior's words all the way to his soul. "Thank--"

Ciara snapped her fingers in front of his eyes. "Wakey, wakey, Jakey. Were you daydreaming or are you drunk? I didn't think the latter was possible, but your eyes are all glazed over and I've been trying to get your attention for a while. I'm looking for Merc but can't find him anywhere."

"Ciara. Love." He pulled her to him and kissed her fast and hard even though their masks went askew and fell off their faces.

Ciara kissed him back matching his fervor, boiling his needs to both protect her and fuck her. A gentle hand through his hair and the way she nuzzled her cheek into the crook of his neck were the only things that stopping him from protesting as she broke their kiss. "I was worried about you. I know that look on your face. You were having a vision."

That didn't sound right. "I was simply talking to a wizened warrior."

She sighed and squeezed him tighter. "Was he dressed like Julius Caesar?"

"Yes." The fact that she hadn't seen him talking to the

warrior but knew what he looked like was enough to sound the alarm. "You can tell me why you know that later. I need to get you out of here."

He picked her up like the princess she was and marched across the garden. Ciara squirmed in his arms and if he wasn't hell bent on locking her in his brand-new state of the art safe room and treasure hoard, he'd enjoy the wiggle of her ass against his cock immensely.

"What? Why? No, no, no. Jakob, I promise we can play all the dirty games you want later, but--"

He was a smart, smart dragon and also had a plush double-king-sized bed installed in the treasure room. "That's a promise you will keep, but you are in danger."

She stopped her writhing, which was almost too bad and scanned the area. A light mist settled just above the heads of the guests as her powers manifested. "Is it demon dragons? Where?"

"I don't know yet what the danger is, but I won't take any chances with you."

Snowflakes with edges like razors formed around Ciara's head like a crown of protection. "We must protect our guests too."

He loved her badass side, but until he knew what was plaguing their party, he wouldn't take any chances with her safety. "As soon as you and the other humans are inside, I will gather all the warriors. We will root out the problem."

"Jakob," Ciara growled in her sexy take-no-shit-from-him kind of way.

"Milacku," he growled right back. He already knew he would lose the battle against her want and need to help him fight the forces of evil. He stopped, set her on her feet and pressed his forehead to hers. "What would you have me do?"

She wrapped her arms around his neck and whispered, "We'll work together. Always together."

They were better together. He knew that but had let fear drive him for too long. "Fine. Don't be obvious but look around at our guests. What do you see?"

Ciara slid her hands down and took one of his in hers. She moved so they were standing side by side and inspected the party like she was a queen surveying her people. "Warriors and humans, talking, flirting, oh, those two are sticking their tongues down each other's throats."

He saw only the same but had noticed the important difference. "Yes, and are any of the dragon's soul shards glowing for having found their mates?"

"Damn. I was afraid of that but didn't want to admit it. Not a single one. I don't believe that's possible. I happen to know there are dragon's mates here tonight. You don't think it could be a coincidence that none of them have found each other yet, do you?" Her tone suggested she didn't think that either but was hoping for an easier explanation.

"My gut tells me it isn't." The power surging through his body knew better. "It's a feeling I haven't been able to shake all night."

Ciara quietly gasped. "Umm, you know how I said your eyes were glazed over and it looked like you were having a vision?" She jerked her chin in the direction of the nearest people to them. "Jakob, look at their eyes, look at everyone's eyes."

"Clever girl." He opened up his senses beyond his weaker human form's and used his dragon eyes to see further into the night. "All of my warriors have that same look. The humans too. Everyone except that man wearing the fruit of the underworld on his mask."

That man was not a dragon, and he wasn't human, or wasn't any longer. Jakob sniffed the air, sorting through the scents of anticipation, disappointment, merry-making, and longing, only to find a common thread of deep, almost rabid, lust. Even the couple nearby making out didn't have that same intoxicating scent.

Jakob's scales rippled over his body, his dragon preparing to rise up and attack this threat. "Incubus."

"Inky-who?"

This sort only ranked a mere step above demon dragons when it came to creatures from hell that Jakob didn't like. "A demon who feeds on blood and the sexual energy of others."

Her eyes narrowed and the ground around their feet began to smoke as tiny fires simmered in the grass. "I did not put any demons on the guest list."

His mate was pissed. He could hardly wait to see her incinerate this particular demon. "He was not invited, and he has outstayed his welcome. Shall we show him the door?"

"Yeah, the door to hell." A gust of wind blew through her hair nearly knocking him over.

Good Gods, she was hot when she was enraged. She took a step forward stomping out the fires sprouting up in her path as she went. Unfortunately, she went in the opposite direction of the Incubus. "You're going the wrong way, dear heart."

"Point me in his direction, because I can't see him at all. Why don't I see him? What did you say he was wearing? Fruit?"

Fleur and Steele approached them. Fleur looked worried

and Steele was literally snarling. "Boss, what the fuck is going on?"

"You scent him too?" Good, at least someone else could vouch that Jakob wasn't just being overprotective of his mate or going crazy.

Fleur wrinkled up her nose. "Incubus stink is my least favorite candle at Rogue Island Candle Company."

"Oh man, is that what I'm smelling? I thought I'd over grown some of the pumpkins and they were rotting. But no one else said anything, so I thought maybe I was smelling my upper lip." Ciara rubbed her nose.

His adorable American mate said the strangest things. "Your upper lip is not only fine, it is delicious. It seems we four are the only ones to recognize his stench."

A deep male voice came from behind them. "Then we should do something about that, don't you think?"

The four of them spun around to see Match, arms folded and a distinct wisp of smoke drifting up from his right nostril. His eyes were deep glowing red, and he was the definition of furious. "After you, little brother."

Match deferred to Jakob, which surprised the shit out of him. He expected the alpha of alphas to immediately take over and direct the battle. Maybe Caesar was right, and the other Wyverns appreciated what Jakob had accomplished even more than he did himself. Dare he even say respect?

Maybe not. The muscle in Match's jaw pulsed as he looked over Jakob's costume. Dude never did have a sense of humor. Although, was that a flicker of humor in his eyes? Nah. Must be his dragon pushing to get out. Jakob calculated he had maybe three minutes before the fiery red dragon took over and torched half his house in the process of incinerating the incubus.

"He hasn't caught on yet that we're on to him. Let's surround him, Dragons behind and to the sides, and you ladies," Jakob winked at his mate, "excuse me, badass witches, from the front. We'll drive him toward you, and you can capture him in a net of vines."

"How about in a giant pumpkin?" Ciara suggested rubbing her hands together, Earth magic sparkling between them.

"Yes, filled with gross, slimy, stringy pumpkin guts." Fleur grinned evilly.

"And if he tries to harm anyone?" Match raised an eyebrow.

"You can light him on fire." Words like music for a red dragon, even the Wyvern. "But I'd rather capture him and question why he's here. I've never known an incubus to interact with demon dragons, but with the addition of the Black Dragon, I think we can't discount that this is another attempt from hell to strike at the Green Dragon Wyr or infiltrate my hoard and get to our relics."

"As much as I hate to allow any demons to live, I agree with your plan, brother. Our enemy is getting smarter. But if demon dragons or the Black Dragon appear, I will use my fire to end them."

Getting Match to resist incinerating first and asking questions later was a major feat all on its own. Red Dragons all have a hate on for any kind of demon, but Match most of all. Which Jakob could use to his advantage. "I'm counting on it."

Jakob, Steele, and Match took up positions around the incubus and it only took a moment for him to notice them closing in on them. His powers were extremely strong. He wasn't just casting his glamour of lust over the people around him, but a wide thin net of it over the entire party. He'd somehow made every single being here see what he wanted them to see but wasn't pushing any of them into a sexual frenzy or even attempting to drink anyone's blood.

He wasn't here to feed, and that made Jakob very wary. Instinct he could understand, but subterfuge except to lure in their prey wasn't typical demon behavior. They would soon find out his end game.

The incubus backed away like the coward he was. He identified Jakob as the point man and narrowed his eyes. "Interesting that you're able to resist my glamour, dragon. That hasn't happened to me in several hundred years or so."

The demon was trying to distract him. Two could play at that game. Jakob stalked forward slowly, keeping the incubus's attention on him, so Ciara and Fleur could spring their trap. "Keep talking, *kurva sac*. We've got lots of questions for you."

A few of the other dragons caught on that Jakob, Steele, and Match were stalking something and had taken up positions to protect the other guests. Merc stepped up just in time to block the demon from escaping into a group of guests who were completely oblivious to the danger nearby.

"Ones that will have to wait for another night. *Zae lunibulungmen*, and you'll pay for it." The demon stepped into the shadow cast by Merc's hulking form and disappeared in a puff of smoke.

What the shit? Incubus didn't use shadow like demon dragons. Merc and Steele exchanged frowns and Match came over and torched the ground where the demon had disappeared. Ciara and Fleur rushed over while no one else around them even noticed the commotion.

"Where did he go?" Ciara knelt and picked up a charred piece of the demon's mask. "Dang it all to hell. I was saving my Peter-Peter-pumpkin eater insult for when we caught him."

"Caught who?" Ky Puru joined the circle around the burnt ground. "What did I miss?"

Ciara examined Ky's face, looking directly into his eyes. Ky winked at her. The dog. "Jakob, I think your mate is flirting with me."

"She is not." Jakob growled and pulled Ciara to his side. His dragon was roaring mine mine mine inside, but he knew she already was his and he was hers. She wore his soul shard after all.

The shard that was not currently glowing. Neither was the one around Fleur's neck. Jakob's dragon roared even louder in his head and pushed to get out and claim his mate. He'd have to settle for nuzzling her neck where his mark decorated her skin for all to see. She was his, damn it.

"I am not. You're flirting with me." Ciara rolled her eyes, but her cheeks were a little flushed. "Look, you guys. His eyes are still glazed. The demon might be gone, but the spell on the dragons hasn't been lifted."

THE POWER OF LOVE

$\mathcal{I}$f ever Ciara needed chocolate, it was now. Chocolate made everything better. Considering her masquerade ball was not only the matchmaking flop of the century, it had been infiltrated by evil spawn from hell, she might make that chocolate in the form of a big ole hunk of THC brownie or other edible. She plopped down on the nearest pumpkin and put her chin in her hands.

Badass Wyvern's mates didn't crawl into bed and cry when things didn't go their way. A lonely wedding planner from a year ago might have done that, but she'd grown since then, fell in love, find out she had magical powers, quit letting her mother poke at her boundaries, and saved her dragon's life.

She stood up and shoved her fist into the air. "I am woman, hear me roar."

Jakob ogled her and said, "I know how to make you roar, sweetheart, but it might make our guests overly jealous."

"I know how to make your roar too, dragon boy. But later. After we figure out how to break the demon's spell over our guests. No nookie until we know everyone else gets to find the love of their lives too." Ciara studied Ky some more who didn't seem to have a care in the world or be bothered by what they were talking about in the least. He did keep making bedroom eyes at her. Some lucky lady was going to fall hard for him.

Match, who clearly was looking for more victims to torch turned to her. "Little mate of the Green Wyvern, are you not a white witch?"

"A. I'm not little, and B. Yes, but I'm still learning how to use my powers." You poop. She didn't say that last part, but she did think it very loudly in his general direction.

"You grumpy ass bastard." Jakob's face lit up. His words were insulting, but his tone of voice was excited, and he made it sound more like a compliment. "That's it. That's the key to breaking the incubus's glamour."

Ciara shook her head and shrugged. "What is, insults? I mean, I can come up with some mean your mama burns, but that's about it."

Jakob chucked her under the chin. "Heart of my heart, light of my soul. You are a white witch, one who controls all four elements. But do you know what happens when you combine the four?"

Match laid a hand on Jakob's arm. "You're treading awfully close to Wyvern secrets that have not been told in centuries, brother. Be sure you know what you are doing."

"I do." Jakob smiled a little cockily and his voice resounded with confidence.

"Good, it's about time. I'm leaving." He nodded to Jakob and then bowed elegantly to Ciara. "Until our next battle, *pierwszy wśród partnerów*."

Match walked a few yards away, shifted into his great red dragon, and flew away into the night.

Ciara put her hands on her hips and made a frowny face at Match's retreating form. "Okay, that was weird, and you'll have to tell me what he said later, but what were you going to say about combining the elements? Is that a thing?"

"Steele, take Fleur and go check on our guests, please. I need to talk to my mate." Steele gave Jakob a salute and walked away. Jakob pulled Ciara over to the side of the house all super secret sneaky like.

"Ooh. Are you going to impart dragony secrets upon me?" She kidded, but hoped he was going to let her a little more into all those places in his head she wasn't yet privy too.

"Yes, *milacku*."

Oh, crap on a cracker, he wasn't kidding. Yay. "Seriously? That's so cool. Hit me with it."

Jakob rubbed his thumb in circles over her collar bone sending all kinds of zings through the dragon mark she had on her skin there. "This information is passed down from Wyvern to Wyvern, father to son. It is a story as old as our people. None of us have ever thought it would come in useful, because there has only ever been the White Witch with the ability to control all four elements."

"Until me?" There was so much to learn about dragon culture and history. She should write a book to help other new mates. Hmm. Maybe later.

"Until you." He confirmed. "When all four elements are combined, they form a fifth element."

"Oh." She almost laughed but held it in since this was serious dragon business. "I think I saw that movie."

Good thing she didn't giggle because Jakob had that sexy-ass dominating I'm-the-Wyvern look on his face. "*Key-ong* is the most powerful element of all."

Huh. Not surprisingly, she hadn't heard of this new element. Thus, why she and other mates were gonna need that handbook. The idea of that project was rapidly climbing up her priority ladder. Number two after saving this masquerade. "You think I have or can create this *key-ong*?"

"I'm sure it's within you. I feel it every time I kiss you, or touch you, or have you under me writhing with pleasure. I feel it now simply looking into your gorgeous eyes." Jakob looked at her so passionately she thought she might erupt into flames or start sprouting flowers all over the place.

She knew what *key-ong* was. She had it in spades. Because of Jakob.

"I think I know what to do. Give me your hand." She slid her hand into her mate's, closed her eyes, and brought up all of her very favorite memories of meeting him, falling in love, the mating ceremony, when he'd given her his soul shard, and every single kiss before and since.

"Yes, that's it. A little more, Ciara. You can do it." He squeezed her hand and his own part of the *key-ong* flowed into her.

The elements swirled inside of her. Earth, Wind, Fire, Water and... there was something more that she couldn't identify, that she hadn't accessed before. Whatever it was, she grabbed onto it and did her best to mash them all together inside of her own heart and soul. Just when she was sure she couldn't contain the power any longer, it trickled out of every pore in her body.

Ciara opened her eyes and created a gentle breeze that picked up the magic and pushed it out and over the garden where all the partygoers were hanging out. The bit of wind hit Ky first and his mask fell off his face and too the ground. He blinked a few times and immediately the glazed look in his eyes cleared.

"Hey, there you are. Have you seen Match yet?"

The wind continued tow swirl through the party, knocking all the masks from everyone's faces and clearing the incubus's spell as it did. Ciara almost jumped up and down and clapped as she spied a glowing green soul shard around the neck of Green Dragon Warrior nearby. The *key-ong* not cleared everyone's eyes, but as it did, the dragons gathered were able to see their fated mates.

Another, and another, and another green glow popped up as more masks were knocked off and soon there were at least a dozen dragons with not only a brightly lit shard, but a mate in their arms. Cheers went up all around the party.

"Well done, my love. I knew you had it in you." Jakob picked her up and spun her in a circle, peppering her face with kisses. He set her down and raised a hand into the air to get everyone's attention. "Three cheers for all the Dragon Warriors who've found their mates tonight, thanks to the greatest Wyvern's mate in the world."

The crowd erupted into hip-hip hoorays and Ciara giggled. "I'm the only Wyvern's mate in the world, you know?"

Jakob pulled her tight against his side. "Yes, you are, and you're all mine."

"I wouldn't have it any other way." She was excited to meet all the new mates and welcome them into the Wyr though.

From out of the corner of her eye, she saw one dragon whose shard was glowing bright, but who was not kissing a newly found mate like there was no tomorrow. "Jakob, you should go congratulate your newly mated warriors and invite them and their new mates to dinner next week. I need to go see to something."

Ciara crossed the garden to the pumpkin carving station where Merc stood poking holes into a poor innocent gourd. "Heya, Merc. Can I see your eyes, please?"

He wasn't wearing a mask, so presumably the *key-ong* wind had made it into the tent too. Merc looked down at Ciara, and while his eyes were clear, there was something else in them that she knew all too well. Disbelief.

Been there, done that, got the scars. Merc didn't believe that whoever his fated mate was would want him, could love him. She couldn't imagine why, but she did understand that everyone had their own inner demons to defeat and they were often worse than any demons sent from hell. But sometimes those inner demons simply needed a stern talking to by someone who cared. "What's going on?"

"What if he doesn't like me? Just because we're fated mates doesn't mean he has to be happy about it." Merc swallowed hard and glanced quickly at the other end of the table.

Ciara took a quick peek just to see who Merc was so afraid of meeting. She ogled the man dressed as Captain America among a throng of Thors. If she didn't know better, she might have thought he actually was Chris Evans. This guy was actually even better looking. Like if Chris Evans and Chris Hemsworth and Chris Pine all had a super baby, it would be Merc's soon to be mate. Lucky duck.

"Okay, I totally get why you might be intimidated by a dude that undeniably H-A-W-T, but Merc, he keeps glancing over here at you. He wants you to go over and talk to him."

"What? No," Merc deflected. "He's probably looking at my penis."

Ciara choke-laughed and then realized Merc pointed to the carving he'd done the day before. She cleared her throat and took Merc by the shoulders. "Listen to me, you big sexy dragon warrior. Even if that guy wasn't your fated mate and probably already half in love with you - I should know - he would fall for you in a second anyway. You're gorgeous AF, you're sweet and kind, while also being a bad-ass warrior and defender of all against the forces of evil. If I weren't mated to your Wyvern, I'd be a little in love with you myself."

"But--"

"No, buts. That guy wants to get in your pants. I've got the worst gaydar on the planet and even I can tell. So, go over there and talk to him. Maybe see if he wants to touch your," she paused for dramatic effect, "penis."

Merc's eyes went wide until Ciara hefted the carved vegetable into his hands. Then she gave him a shove in the direction of Captain America's Ass. She watched as Merc's soul shard went haywire and both men's cheeks went pink. Aww. Perfect.

Her matchmaking work done she could now rejoin and enjoy the rest of the party. She looked around for Jakob, but her cell phone rang in her pocket. That was weird, she didn't even remember this dress having pockets. Bonus.

She pulled her phone out and saw Wesley's name on the screen. She swiped and answered. "Where did you get off to? You missed my brilliant matchmaking skills."

"So sorry I couldn't make your party, sugar. You know how your mother is." Wesley's baritone came through the line crisp and clear, but there was definitely a Halloween themed wedding happening in the background.

Wait? What? Ciara didn't get a chance to ask because Wes barreled right over her.

"Not that she needed to worry. The new girl at work, Heather, is simply divine. You'd like her, she's smart, savvy, likes to read romance books, and I think you should send one of your dragon hotties over for her. She's got the curves like those dragons love. I'm sure she'd light up any man dragon's pants, oh, I mean soul shard."

"Are you punking me right now? Have you been watching Ashton Kutcher prank people on YouTube again?" She would see if they could send a few more dragon warriors over to America because there were a lot of amazeballs women there for them to romance. But that didn't explain why Wes was apologizing for not being at the party.

"Gotta run, doll face. Your mother is on the hunt. Just wanted to check in and make sure your party was the bomb-diggity you hoped for. Ciao." He hung up and Ciara stared at her phone frowning for longer than was strictly necessary.

If Wes hadn't come over for the party, then who the hell was that guy who'd pretended to be him? She stomped her foot. Dog gone it. He must have been the incubus. Grr. She was going to get Match to blow fire up that guy's ass again the next time they saw him. She marched over to Jakob, Ky, Steele, and Fleur to tell them about her discovery.

Mrs. Bohacek in a toga joined her on her walk. "What's wrong, dear? Demons got you down?"

"How did he fool me? The bastard." Icicles formed on the cuffs and hem of Ciara's dress and she had to shake them off.

"Don't worry too much about him or his sister. They'll be a

pain in some other dragon's ass soon enough. You did well tonight."

Uh-oh. That didn't sound good. Ciara knew better than ask her to clarify. She'd never get a straight answer out of Mrs. B. "Thanks. How come you didn't tell me about *key-ong*?"

Mrs. B. winked at Julius Caesar as they walked by. "That's something everyone has to discover for themselves, we can but show them they are loved when they are on that journey of self-discovery. Remember that later down the road in the dark times to come."

"I don't like the sound of that." Now that more of the Green Dragons Warriors were finding mates, it should be happy times ahead.

"Love isn't always easy," Mrs. Bohacek took Ciara's hands in hers and with each word, her form faded like a hologram or a ghost, "but I'm counting on it to conquer all."

Aha. She was right about where *key-ong* came from. But, umm, just to make sure, she asked, before Mrs. B disappeared and since she seemed to be in an answering sort of mood. "Love?"

"What do you think *key-ong* is?" And with that, she popped out of existence leaving Ciara with a handful of nothing in her palms.

Jakob waved to her and she finally pushed her way through the revelers to her mate's side once again. "*Milacku*, you haven't seen Cage, have you?"

"Not since before the kerfuffle with the Incubus. You don't think something happened to him, do you? What if the spell wasn't broken for him?" Ciara liked Cage and would hate for anything bad to happen to him.

Ky smirked. "Nah. He's probably off romancing some sex-on-a-stick. Not like any dragons besides the greens had their soul shards light up tonight anyway."

"Okay. Oh, I just had the most interesting conversations with... somebody." That was weird. Who had she been talking to? "About King Kong or maybe it was Qui-Gon Jinn, or something about a key gong?"

Jakob and Ky exchanged looks that said they thought she was drunk. "Maybe I should take you up to bed, my mate. You've had a long and exciting day."

"But we're in the middle of the party and we've got guests." She waved her hand toward the people having fun around them. "We can't abandon our own party half-way through."

Jakob raised one eyebrow in that sexy I'm-the-boss-and-will-think-of-a-way-to-get-you-into-bed way he had. He turned to Steele. "You are in charge for the remainder of the evening. Do not disturb us unless there is another demon attack, and only then if you feel you can't handle it on your own."

"You got it, boss." Steele saluted. "Fleur and I are happy to step in as substitute hosts."

Ciara checked with Fleur quickly, who nodded back and waved her off. "Have fun. Don't do anything I wouldn't do. Or do, because that could be fun, and you can tell me all about it over pumpkin scones for breakfast tomorrow morning."

Jakob picked Ciara up and threw her over his shoulder. She didn't protest once because she was too distracted by the way his butt moved in his tight red leather pants. They disappeared into his office where he punched a code into a hidden keypad and a door swished open.

"Where are we going?" She knew he had a new hiding spot for his treasure hoard, but she hadn't gotten to see it yet.

He entered a room, the door shut automatically behind them, and the lights went out dropping them into complete darkness. The next thing she knew, Jakob had shifted into his dragon form and was carrying her cradled in his great talons as he flew down some kind of long pitch-black corridor. *Welcome to my lair, fair princess.*

A light appeared at the end of the tunnel and inside was a room with a huge, enormous, gigantic bed. It was absolutely beautiful. Especially the sparkling jack-o-lantern bejeweled with citrine and emeralds sitting on the headboard. He set her carefully on the end of the mattress and picked up the price-less piece of Halloween art in his claws. He held it out to her. "Aw, did you make that for me?"

Jakob shifted back into his dragon form, but this time, he wasn't wearing any clothes. He stalked toward. "I told you Green Dragons are skilled at vegetable artistry."

Ciara carefully set the pumpkin back on the headboard and stripped out of her dress. "I can see that. What else are big bad Green Dragon Warriors are good at?"

"Loving our amazing gorgeous sumptuous mates." Jakob pressed her back into the soft green blankets, spreading her legs and pushing himself between them.

"Show me, dragon of mine."

And he did. All night long... and for the rest of their lives.

READ JAKOB and Ciara's full-length novel Chase Me if you haven't yet!

Or get the next book in the Dragons Love Curves series where Ky Puru finds his fated mate in Bite Me!

SURPRISE ME

DRAGONS LOVE CURVES BOOK 6.5

CASTLES IN THE SKY

*J*ett was beyond fucking stressed. A year ago, he didn't even know that word much less what it felt like. Yeah, most of his life had been shitty, but stress was not in his vocabulary. Being deemed the head of a brand-new Dragon Wyr and finding out who his real parents were came with all kinds of responsibilities he certainly wasn't prepared for.

Who would have thought being the Demon Dragon Wyvern came with so much god-damned paperwork?

He scribbled his name on yet another form and shoved it into a pile to be mailed. Why the hell he couldn't just take over some foreign castle for the new Demon Dragon home was beyond him. It's not like anyone was using the dilapidated buildings he wanted to buy. He'd be doing the country a favor by fixing them up.

Red tape had become his second worst nightmare.

"Jett? What are you doing up? Come to bed." Yvaine leaned against the doorway to the office Jett had procured in this little German town. Their sleep schedules still weren't quite in sync. She was a creature of light and got tired when it was dark out. He could occasionally coax her out when the moon shined bright, but most of the time she went to bed early and rose early. The sun was just about to come up, and she looked sleepy and rumpled.

Too bad it wasn't because they'd had a tumble in the sheets together. He'd skip sleep for a thousand days in a row to be with her. One more day wouldn't hurt him. "Filing the paperwork the government wants, love. Nothing to worry about."

She yawned and stretched, every plump luscious curve on her gorgeous body emphasized with each movement. Her sleep shirt, with a unicorn drinking a cup of coffee on it, did nothing to hide those hips and thighs he loved so much. Yvaine crossed over to him and he welcomed her to curl up in his lap. Her head on his shoulder, she sleepily asked, "Did you find us a place to live?"

Her fingers wandered down his shirt and she lazily reached underneath and circled the skin around his belly button. Even that simple touch did good things to soothe his stress and ramp up his need for her. He could forget about all his worries if he bent her over the desk and lost himself in her body. For now running his fingers along her bare soft skin would have to suffice.

"Maybe." If the damn bureaucrats would let him go fucking buy the place. Civil servants could give demon wyrms a run for their money when it came to driving Jett crazy. Fucking bastards.

"Does it have lots of places to run, hide, and play games?" Her voice was either husky from sleep or she was imagining the same kinds of games Jett was. Naked, dirty games.

"Only a castle and its extensive grounds and forests will do for you." Nothing was as good as he wanted it to be for her. She deserved a Disney castle with shining white walls and pink flags flying from the turrets. He was going to give her a run-down pile of bricks and he felt like shit about it. He and his brethren would work for years to make it a home for them all. A place where they could be safe and not disturb the humans while they trained and learned to use their power over the shadow. No one would go looking for dragons and a unicorn in a UNESCO world heritage site.

"Cool." She yawned again and tried to get up, but Jett pulled her back down and sneaked a hand between her warm thighs. She chuckled and slapped his hand away. "Let's go play some of those games after I get back from Spain."

"Spain?" What was Cage up to bringing Jett's mate into Gold Wyr territory? He already had a whole team of Jett's best Demon Dragon Warriors working for him. Now the asshat wanted his mate too. Jett didn't like that one bit.

"Azy has invited me to the twins' birthday party. I've never been to one and I so want to be BFFs with the other Wyvern mates. They're all going." Her fingers walked their way down to the button on his jeans. "You'll take me, won't you?"

Fuck. He could never say no to her. But he couldn't take a day off right now to go...do whatever happens at birthday parties. More Demon Dragon Warriors were appearing out of the depths of hell each day and they had to be brought into the fold of the Wyr. Plus, everyone was still learning to use their powers and he would not leave their training to anyone else. Dammit. "Even if you stick your hands down my pants, I can't take you. I'll assign a team to escort you if it's that important that you go. But just for the day. I want you back by nightfall."

His Demon Dragon Warriors would fight any wyrms to the death to protect Yvaine. The muscles in his chest clenched. Jett couldn't take any chances that the Black Dragon might come for her.

"Have you ever had a birthday party?" She looked up and her sparkling violet eyes were filled with curiosity and so much love it made his heart skip a beat.

Jett didn't even have any idea how old he or when he was born was thanks to Ereshkigal's curse. He'd never even had a birthday, much less a party. Not a whole lot of celebrating in hell. Except for Fallyn's gruesome birthday presents the past hundred years or so. He doubted Cage and Azy were going to strike their children with a hellfire whip for each year old they were.

"No, sunshine." He couldn't even imagine celebrating the passing of his years. He'd much rather mark the passing of time since he'd met Yvaine. That seemed much more fitting of a party than his birth.

"Me either." She shrugged. Something in her voice hinted that she didn't want him to think that bothered her. "Time doesn't pass the same in *Tir na nog*, so no birthdays for me. That I remember anyway."

Wait, what? If anyone's birth should be celebrated it was that of his Yvaine. "But you weren't born there. When is your birthday?"

She shook her head as if it didn't matter and played with the button on his pants. "I don't know. Cait of the *Sith* only gave me a hint. I know my mother died when I was born and that was in 1179. When is yours?"

Yvaine didn't look up at him and flicked the tab on his zipper. She was trying to distract him, so he didn't notice she cared about this. Good try. Nothing about Yvaine slipped past him. She was his life, his soul, his soulmate and he'd do everything in his power to make her happy. But he didn't know how to fix this. "I think I'm much older than you, but I don't know either."

"That stinks. Now I'm depressed. You should probably do something to make me feel better." She waggled her eyebrows at him and wiggled her bare ass across his lap.

Jett picked Yvaine up by the waist and set her ass on the edge of his desk, so she had to spread her legs to make room for him. If ever he needed an excuse for a break, making his soul mate happy was it. He slipped his jeans down past his hips and pressed his erection against her, teasing her clit with the tip. "I see what you're doing, love of my life. I will distract you from this pain in your heart for now. But know that your pain is my pain and we will work together to solve any problem. Okay?"

Yvaine tilted her hips so their bodies were ready to join and wrapped her ankles around his waist. "I love you, you big broody dragon."

Still avoiding, but he'd let her have that for now. "I will love you for always and ever."

They took each other fast and hard at first. When her small cries of pleasure told him she was close to coming, he slowed, wanting to draw her orgasm out as long as he could. "Come for me, Yvaine. Let me feel your body begging for mine."

"Yes, you're mine, Jett." She arched her back and dug her feet into his ass. Her inner muscles clenched down on him in a rhythm so luscious he couldn't hold himself back any longer.

Jett lowered his mouth to her shoulder, ripped the fabric of her nightgown with his teeth and licked the soft flesh where the mark of the demon dragon writhed on her skin. A warm glow spread through his chest, a heat that he felt only when he was with her. Jett thrust into her tight body once more and bit down, sending them both into nirvana. Which was his favorite place to be with her.

They held each other for a long time, breathing hard and coming back to reality. That's when Yvaine started giggling. She laughed hard enough that her whole body shook and since Jett was still buried deep inside of her, he didn't mind her titters even a little bit. In fact, she was getting him hard all over again.

"What's so funny?" Her sweetness and light dug so far into his dark soul that even he couldn't help but smile.

It took her another second to get a hold of herself before she could speak. She smiled up at him and then ran a hand along his jaw. "How come you're so freaking good at that?"

He loved this time spent in her arms and didn't ever want it to end. Jett pulled up the dragon to shift just his wings and wrapped them around the two of them to block out the rays of the rising sun and the world just a little bit longer. "At what, love?"

One more giggle slipped out. "Making my eyes roll back in my head until I can see stars with my skin."

"You mean fucking you into oblivion?" That was a skill he enjoyed very, very much. "Say it, Yvaine. Tell me I fucked your brains out."

"You flookered my brains out." Yvaine wrinkled up her

nose. "You flicker-flacked my brains out. You flagenshchoop-ered my brains out."

This was one of his all-time favorite games. One he had yet to win. "Close enough. I've worked up quite an appetite flagenschoopering you. Let me make you breakfast before you head off to the party."

Yvaine kissed him on the nose, dragged him to the kitchen and ended up making breakfast for them both. Jett was almost getting used to her vegan meat substitutes. She laid three strips of tofurkey bacon in front of him.

Nope. Kidding. Who knew dragons had a gag reflex? Those were still disgusting, and he'd settle for some black coffee until she was gone, and he could eat a couple of pounds of good German pork sausage.

While they ate, or rather Yvaine did, Jett messaged three Demon Dragon Warriors to accompany her on the quick flight. They were some of the best FNGs he had and were all ready to become lieutenants for him. As soon as Neo got back from his mission to help root out the demon wyrms in Dubai they'd start including these guys in the inner workings of the Wyr.

When they walked in Yvaine winked at them and offered them bacon. One reached for a slice, but Jett shook his head in warning. She popped it into her mouth and scooted behind Jett so they didn't see her naked ass. "Your loss, boys. I'll just run upstairs and change for this shindig. Does anyone know what one wears to a birthday party?"

They all shook their heads.

"Well, you're no help at all. I'll be back down in a jiffy or two." She kissed Jett on the cheek and stole his coffee as she left the room.

Jett poured more for himself and his warriors. He handed the brew out and leaned against the table. "Yvaine needs to go to the Gold Wyr headquarters. You three will accompany her through the shadow on her journey."

The Warriors nodded solemnly. Good. They understood the importance of their mission. Not only were they going to protect Yvaine, they were emissaries into another Wyr's territory. These three would be on their best behavior.

"I'm entrusting Yvaine's life in your hands, Warriors. Don't take your eyes off her for even a second," he said to the biggest of the three.

The Warrior set his cup down and crossed his arms. "We won't. We will give our lives for hers if needs be."

"Thank you, brother." Jett clasped the Warrior's arm. "And see if she can help you choose names while you're together."

Each of their eyes looked hopeful. They chorused a, "Yes, sir."

The moment they were away, Jett texted a half-dozen more warriors. This group were solid, but not quite up to the skill level of the ones he'd sent with Yvaine. Their fighting prowess wouldn't matter as much for the project he had for them. When they'd all gathered, looking stern and foreboding, he prepared them for their mission.

"Warriors, I have a very important task for you. It's one I wish I could do myself, but I have to meet with some government officials to try and procure our new home. You are some of the brightest minds in our Wyr and I trust you with the happiness of my mate."

The warriors stood up taller, alert, and ready for battle. They were going to need every bit of strength they had for this task.

"You six will investigate and research how to throw a birthday party for Yvaine. I need to fly over to the property I hope we'll call home soon and I'm counting on you to accomplish this task in my absence."

"What's a birthday?" the closest one asked.

MY SUPER SWEET BIRTHDAY DISASTER

*S*hit. Maybe this wasn't a good idea.

His Warriors did need to learn to live in the human world if their Wyr was going to be trusted to fight alongside the other Dragons Warriors. "This mission will not only be a favor to me and Yvaine, but a good way for you to learn to assimilate into the human world. If you don't know what a birthday is, I expect you to find out."

Not like he had a lot of answers for them anyway. Whatever they presented to him would be a learning experience for him too. "I'll be back tonight, you can give me your first findings then."

Jett left for the upper middle Rhine Valley using the shadow to get there in only moments. He took his time scouting around the forested area around the castle he planned to buy. Out of all the castles and manor houses he'd looked at, this was his first choice. The Sauerburg was smack dab in the middle of a UNESCO World Heritage site and that would keep other builders or developers at bay. Plus, there was a cool-ass tower he and his brethren could take flight from and land on in the dark of night.

It wasn't like he hadn't offered the government here enough money. Three million Euro would make a dent in his treasure hoard. Fine. He would replenish it with the veins of gold running deep underground all throughout the area. Living underground in the depths of hell most of his life had to have some advantages. Being able to sniff out gold deep below the Earth's crust was one of them.

The bureaucrats kept Jett busy for far longer than he hoped and the only thing that kept him from lighting each and every one of them on fire were the selfies Yvaine sent him throughout the day at the birthday party. She had very creative uses for her tongue in those pictures. Plus, he got a teensy glimpse of some of the activities at this kind of party. He filed face-painting and balloons away in his mental files for what to do at her birthday celebration.

He was especially interested in the part where people were blindfolded and beating some paper beast with a stick. Yvaine looked especially delicious blindfolded. With that thought, he ended the meeting so he could get back to her. "Gentlemen. Final offer. Three million Euro, with an investment of another five million over the next five years into renovations, restoration, and upkeep. That should invigorate your local economy and line your pockets. Take it or leave it. I'll give you until next week to make your decision as I will be busy celebrating my wife's birthday until then. You can contact my office with the paperwork."

He left the greedy slimeballs with their jaws hanging open and headed back into the forest to find a bit of shadow to ride home. He popped back up in the common room in the gasthaus he'd rented out for the Demon Dragon Warriors to live hoping to find birthday plans well underway.

What he found were six dragons sitting around a television with a stack of beer bottles a meter high. Jett had to work really hard to keep the fire from pouring out of his mouth instead of his question. "What in the hell are you doing?"

"Like, Oh my god. You scared the crappola out of us, boss." The nearest Warrior jumped up from the couch.

"Why do you speak like that, Warrior?" Jett growled. He didn't like the tone or the way the warrior said any of the words. This was not how a Demon Dragon spoke. If Ereshkigal had found a way to cast a new spell on his Wyr, Jett was skipping all future celebrations and going straight back down to hell to murder her in the face.

The man swallowed hard and pointed to the TV. On it was a girl in a giant poofy pink dress, wearing a tiara, and riding in a carriage shaped like a swan. She was crying and waving to a crowd of similarly dressed girls. Pink was not in the Black Witch's wardrobe much less her spellwork. The catastrophe on the television reminded him more of a white witch's magic. "What is this? You're supposed to be researching Yvaine's birthday party."

"We so are." The Warrior Jett had left in charge stood up. "This is a very useful American documentary about women's birthday parties. We like literally know exactly what to do to have the most ah-mazing super sweet sixteenth birthday party now."

Another warrior tossed an empty beer bottle at this Warrior's head. "No way. I thought we decided to throw a *quinceanera* instead. Their dresses are so much more fabulous."

Jett glared at the show the men were watching. He wanted to trust that his warriors weren't bespelled. He took in a full three minutes before he knew he was in real trouble. As Yvaine would say, holy forking shirt. This wasn't any magic he could defend against. It was American television.

He'd created monsters. Demon Dragons who'd learned to be human from a television show filled with entitled American teenaged girls were going to be hard to live with. Add a reform program to his list of to-dos. Shit.

"How long have you all been studying this show?" Jett stared each of the Warriors down and they erupted into chatter.

"Pretty much since you left. It was one of the first things we found on the internet when we searched for unicorn birthday parties." The first warrior showed Jett a tablet filled with screenshots of poofy pink dresses.

"No. You forgot about Esty. We can get so many decorations and party favors there. We just need your credit card, boss." The second warrior held out his hand.

Yeah. No.

"We cannot get the volcano like Alyson had at her party on Etsy. That is going to have to be special ordered and you know we need the volcano." The third warrior banged a fist against his hand pretty damn animate about that.

"Dude, we have to support small local businesses." One of the other warriors waved his hand at the tablet again. "Do you know what a fifteen-hundred-dollar cake order would mean to a local bakery?"

Jett blinked a few times and then slowly backed out of the room. This was way worse than he even imagined. He found a corner of shadow and escaped the birthday dragon mayhem.

Okay. So that was a mistake. He would have to be much more careful about what kind of television his newer warriors were allowed to watch.

He made his way back to his office and sat down shaking his head. He got a text from Yvaine saying the party was ending and she would be back in an hours. Just enough time for him to do his own research on birthday parties. The internet was indeed full of useful information and if he couldn't find something there, he would call in reinforcements. He had someone in mind that might actually be able to help, but that would be a last resort.

He searched for sexy woman birthday and the first link he clicked on had more moaning and groaning than anything else. No one else would be allowed to see Yvaine's exposed body this way. No way was he throwing this kind of party. Well, maybe a very private party where he and Yvaine were the only ones invited to come.

Jett tipped his head to the side and stared at the video on this strange site called PornParty. How did that woman do that with her mouth?

One of the three warriors who Jett had sent with Yvaine appeared out of the shadows in Jett's office. He arrived in a warrior's stance and scanned the room. Jett shut the laptop and cut off the end of the sexy woman birthday. The Warrior saluted Jett and then disappeared back into the shadow. Good. They were scouting ahead to make sure her landing point was secure. He knew he'd chosen the right Warriors to guard her.

He felt the tiny vibrations in the air around him that indicated Yvaine was close. In another second the same Warrior popped out of the shadow again followed by Yvaine, flanked by the other two men. She put her hand on her stomach for a second and held up a finger.

"Yvaine, are you okay? Have my warriors failed in their mission? Are you injured?" Jett's dragon shimmered near the surface ready to burst forth and protect his mate. "I'll kill whoever did this to you."

Yvaine looked at him, her eyes wide and then belched, loudly. Pink vapor puffed out of her mouth and she made a face. "Shadow and birthday cake do not mix."

"No incidents to report, sir. The trip was successful." The largest of the three Warriors, who was covered in some kind of yellow sparkling sugar dust stepped up to report.

Jett gave them each a once over and narrowed his eyes. "No incidents? Well done. Thank you for protecting my mate today. You may return to your regular duties."

The Warriors looked pleased at his praise, each of them straightening up and squaring their shoulder after what had to be a trying day if the state of their clothes was any indication. Besides the yellow glitter that seemed to be everywhere, one had a smear from chest to knee of something flakey that smelled of burnt sugar, and the other was missing one sleeve of his shirt and he had a smeared, colorful, childlike drawing of a dragon on his exposed arm.

Yvaine grinned. "Yeah. If you don't count Mr. Glitterface here being attacked by mermaids for taking the pinata candy from a baby."

The Warrior shrugged and didn't seem the least bit sorry. "I didn't take it. She gave it to me."

Jett narrowed his eyes at the Warriors but dismissed them. "Go home, get some rest."

The men filed out and at the last second Jett realized they

were all headed toward the gasthaus. Quickly, under his breath, he warned the last in line. "I'd avoid the common room tonight if I were you. I think you've had enough birthday party for one day."

Mr. Glitterface's eyes went wide and he nodded. "I'm afraid to even ask."

Jett clapped him on the back and returned to the office where Yvaine was stripping. What a perfect way to end a long ass day. He sidled up beside her and reached to help her pull her pants down.

Yvaine held up a hand. "Don't touch me, I think there are ants in my pants. They're like the teensiest dragons burning me everywhere."

She peeled the rest of her clothes off and she was indeed covered in lots of tiny red dots. He touched one and was surprised by its texture. That wasn't skin. He pulled his finger away and the red splotch stuck to him. It glittered when he moved it, not unlike his own scales. "Sweetheart, you don't have ants. This is some kind of plastic or paper or something."

"Fire paper, or paper with teeth. I itch everywhere." Yvaine rubbed at her arms, legs, and stomach and more of the red dots fell to the floor. As they fluttered to the ground, the paper ignited and sparked like miniature fireworks. Only ash hit the floor.

Yvaine sneezed and the rest of the red stuff exploded off of her and shimmered as it too ignited, lighting her up in a twinkling halo. "Whatever it is, I think I'm allergic to it. It must have come out of the pinata."

"Come on then, let's get you into the shower and I'll wash you from head to toe. You can tell me all about the birthday party and I'll tell you about the castle I'm buying you."

The two of them did very little talking in the shower, unless "Don't come until I tell you to," and "more, please, more, yes," counted. Jett also found out exactly how birthday girls liked to use their tongues too.

His lovely mate did seem more tired tonight than usual and he wrapped her up in a big fluffy towel and carried her to their bedroom. She only protested for a second and then curled up in his arms and snored softly. Jett decided to crawl into bed with her for a while and ended up falling asleep too where he dreamed of fiery red glitter and exploding volcano birthday cakes.

"*J*ett. Wake up. Your tail is poking me."

He snorted awake. *Yvaine? Why are we on the floor?*

"You broke the bed. What in the world were you dreaming about that you shifted into your dragon?" Yvaine nuzzled her cheek against the scales on his face and the black and red swirls of magic that signaled his shift encircled them both. In another breath, her skin scraped across the scruff on his chin instead of his protective armor.

"Sorry, love. I dreamed you were in danger, I think. It had something to do with a birthday cake on fire."

"Silly dragon. I guess we both have birthdays on the brain. I was dreaming that you were a giant dragon pinata but instead of being filled with candy, you were empty, and I had to fill you up, but nothing would stay in even though I tried all your favorite flavors of M&Ms."

Damn, he fucking loved her so hard. "You have filled me up with your love. I was so empty before you came into my life."

Yvaine got a sloppy grin on her face. "Holy hobknockers, Jett. Have I told you how corny you are and how much I love it?"

Dragon Warriors were not corny. Except maybe when it came to loving their mates. But, shh, don't tell anyone. "I'm not corny, you're horny."

She giggled in a way that went straight to his cock. She was thinking dirty thoughts. "That gives me an idea for a birthday present for you. But how in the world will I know when to give it to you if you don't know your birthday?"

Jett didn't feel inspired by very many things, but Yvaine was one of them. "Let's just make them up. How about if we give each other birthdays, love. You decide when mine is, and I'll pick yours."

Yvaine rubbed her nose against his and smiled. "I love it. I pick, umm, tomorrow."

"Now, now. Wait just a second, don't tell me, let's make it a surprise. I need time to prepare your presents." He wanted to make sure her birthday party was special and not half-assed.

"Oh. Then, kidding." Her eyes flicked back and forth as she considered something. "I have a better idea. Let's throw each other birthday parties and that's how we'll know when it is."

That fit in perfectly with the plan hatching in Jett's mind. "Good. It's a plan. Now we have that settled--" he flipped her on her back and spread her legs with his knees. "Let's celebrate."

And they did. Three times.

The next couple of days Yvaine spent on the phone and wouldn't let him get close enough to hear who she was talking to or what she was saying. But he was half demon and had ways of finding things out. Like hiding in the shadow so she couldn't see him. Unfortunately, she knew him too well and could hide in the veil between their world and *Tir na Nog*. The sneak.

He did catch her once by leaving out a bowl of ice cream with sprinkles on top when he knew she was hiding nearby. She couldn't resist rainbow sprinkles. He heard her talking on the phone and ask Ciara, the Green Wyvern's mate for help planning, before she caught on to his ploy.

Okay. So, she had brought in a professional party planner for help and he was still stuck with his Warrior yahoos. Great. He wasn't yet ready for his last resort. But he needed to ask for help. Shit. He hated asking for help.

He'd rather call in a favor.

He knew just the dragon to call. Jett had Cage on speed-dial these days.

"What do you want, Jett?" Cage was a grumpy bastard since he became the AllWyvern. Jett couldn't blame him. Just being the leader of one Dragon Wyr was tough enough. It had to be about a billion times worse having the responsibility of all Dragonkind on his shoulders. Not to mention the added stress of Ereshkigal and the Black Dragon being after his kids.

Jett shivered. He was nowhere near ready to even think about having children. What the fuck did he know about being a dad. No, no. That was going to have to wait a long, long time. Millenia.

Always best to get straight to the point with Cage. "I'm calling in a favor."

Cage snorted. "Pretty sure I'm all paid up."

That was true. Jett had called in every favor he'd built up over years garnering when he'd found Yvaine and they'd broken Ereshkigal's curse over his brethren. "Not if I send you the Demon Dragon Warriors you've been begging me for to help you find Geshtianna."

Cage didn't need to know Jett had already sent Neo and some of his best warriors to take out their common enemy. Jett's Demon Dragon Warriors weren't ready to battle the demon wyrms or the Black Dragon. They needed time to recover and create their own lives. But he could spare a few of the stronger Warriors to go hunt out Geshtianna. She would pay for her sins, and the Demon Dragons would be happy to help with that.

Cage harrumphed. "I want those Warriors. What are your terms?"

This was like taking pinata candy from a baby. "Nothing to complicated. I simply need some information and possibly some resources."

"Like what?" Cage's tone was wary.

Time to go in for the kill. "I want to throw Yvaine a birthday party, but I don't know shit about birthdays or parties. Give me some tips and your resources and we'll call it even."

Cage laughed for a full minute. Either he thought Jett was ridiculous or the Gold Wyvern knew that this task was impossible. "You're in deep, man. A birthday party for your mate. Wish I would have thought of that. Kids sure, but not the love of my life."

Okay. So, neither ridiculous nor undoable. Good. "If I can figure out how to get this shit done, all the Wyverns and their mates will be invited."

"Great, so Azy can beat my ass for not throwing her a party." Cage's voice went from AllWyvern and guarded to relaxed. "Why don't you call Ciara? She spent an eternity and half my fortune throwing the twins' party yesterday."

Like he hadn't already thought of that. "Can't. Yvaine's got her on speed dial."

"Watch your bank account." Cage laughed. "If I didn't know better, I'd think that woman was a Gold Dragon with how much she likes to spend money."

Good to know. "I don't even know where to start planning a birthday party. Cake. That's all I've got. I know we have to have a cake."

He wasn't going to mention the volcano.

"I wasn't in on most of it, but Ciara and Azy did send me over to a party supply store in America about a half dozen times. The women who run the shop are cute and very helpful."

Hmm. If it wasn't like the TV show his warriors had been watching maybe he could enlist these shopkeepers for help. "Great. Send me the name and address."

A link to Poof the Party Store, in Rogue, New York popped up on his screen. Jett checked the time. It was still late in the States, so he'd have to wait a few hours before he grabbed the party crew and took them on this scouting mission to the shop. Fine. That gave him some time to research and make sure he wasn't walking into a real-life episode of Birthdays Gone Wild.

The shop had a website and Jett surfed around for unicorn birthday items. There were several glittery items that Yvaine would definitely approve of and zero volcanos. He added several things to his cart for pick up when they arrived. Early afternoon he went and woke up the Super Sweet crew to take with him. They had to be good for something. At least they could carry the supplies and hide them in the gasthaus when they returned.

America was a long way to travel through the shadow and there could be perils along the way. Demon wyrms hadn't spent much time plaguing the Americas until recently. The more the Black Dragon sought mates, the more his demon spawn spread across the Earth hunting them. "Be prepared for battle, Warriors."

The six of them nodded and stepped into the shadow one by one headed toward their destination across the ocean. It took several stops in various parts of Hell to get to the States. They didn't run into a single demon, wyrm or otherwise, along the way. That had to mean an ambush.

They emerged out of the shadows in a forested area controlled by the local wolf pack, in their dragon forms, ready for battle. Unless they cooing birds in the trees were demons in disguise, there wasn't going to be a battle today. Jett shifted into his human form and examined the darkness of the woods. The hair on the back of his neck stood on end, but he couldn't sense anything from hell near or far.

He would be much less worried if they had come across an entire horde of the cursed demons formerly known as their brothers in arms. The forces of hell's numbers had been decimated when he and Yvaine broke the curse on Jett's brethren, but even with a tenth of their numbers gone, there should still be plenty around to stalk them through hell and attack.

Where the fuck were all the stinking little bastards?

The Warriors also shifted when no impending danger threatened. They might suck at party planning, but were further along in their training than he'd assumed and moved together like a well-honed machine. They kept him surrounded as the group walked toward the town, even though he'd prefer to run point. His days of sacrificing himself had come to an end when he'd taken on the mantle of Wyvern. Still, he would not allow any of this team to die for him.

Didn't look like they'd have to today anyway. As soon as he got back from this shopping expedition, Jett would contact Cage again and exchange intel on the disappearance of demon wyrms and the Black Dragon. Kur-Jara was up to something.

One more look into the shadow wouldn't hurt. At the edge of town, Jett stopped and sunk back into the trees. "I've got a bad feeling about this, boys. Let's check one more time for demon wyrm activity. Use all your senses to see if they're hiding here. Scout the city and meet back up in the basement of the party store."

One by one they appeared out of the shadows and into the room that was clearly used for storage. Each reported no hint of demon wyrms.

"Good. But keep alert and try not to draw attention to yourselves."

One of the warriors knocked over a small stack of boxes and bags of multi-colored glitter exploded, covering him in a rainbow of sparkles.

"Aww, you look just like my honeypie, young Warrior. It's a good look for you." A beautiful woman with glowing olivy-brown skin, wearing a flowing white dress sat on the bottom step of the staircase leading up to the shop as if she'd been waiting for them. "Well, you boys better come upstairs. The shop girls are waiting for you. They have your order all packed and ready."

Ah shit. What the hell was the White Witch doing at the party supply store?

The words 'shop girls are waiting for you' had the Warriors scrambling to get past her and up to the store's main floor. Each and every member of his Wyr were hoping that the next woman they met might be their soulmate.

"Inanna." Jett greeted her coolly. Their relationship was... tumultuous. The White Witch had helped him and Yvaine find each other, but she wasn't happy about it. She didn't like him. Not that he could blame her. He was the bastard child of her mate and a demon from hell.

She gave a little dip of her head to acknowledge him. "Jett."

"What are you doing in America? There aren't very many of your dragon sons on this side of the pond. Not much matchmaking for you to do." He couldn't help but wonder if she would help his own Demon Dragon Warriors find their mates as she did with the rest of the Wyrs. Probably not. They would have to forge their own way.

She smiled like she knew something he didn't. Which of course she did, she was a goddess. "Oh, you'd be surprised by all the pies I have my fingers in."

Was that supposed to sound dirty? His father must be nearby. The two of them were cringeworthy when it came to being corny about their love and lust for each other. At least Jett knew where he gotten that particular attribute from.

"Want to help me plan Yvaine's birthday party?" The White Witch might not like Jett, but she had a soft spot for Yvaine.

"I'm looking forward to seeing what you can do. I'm only here for a moment to see you anyway." She looked around like she expected someone else to appear.

Him? That was unexpected.

"What can I do for you?" That came out a little more surprised than he'd meant.

"Do you know where Fallyn, is?" Her eyes were sad and worried.

Whoa. Jett assumed the White Witch pretty much knew where everyone in the whole world was at any given time. The fact that he couldn't find Fallyn, the woman he'd basically grown up with in hell, was... interesting. "Have you checked the Christmas ornament store?"

"You're a smart ass." She narrowed her eyes at him. "It's so hard to dislike you when you're so much like your father."

"Thanks? Sorry, I haven't seen Fallyn since our escape from Hell with Azy. I've been a little busy." As she would know. Probably. The pedestal he'd put the White Witch on was a little crooked today.

"Your mate has," she said. One eyebrow went up challenging him to deny it.

Shit. The red sparkly stuff that had made Yvaine all itchy. He knew it seemed somehow familiar. "Fallyn must have been at the twins' birthday party."

"Hmm. Yes. Well, then maybe I will help you with your party, so she'll come to that as well." Inanna waved her hand and a heard of elephants - or Demon Dragon Warriors - crashed around upstairs. "There that should do it."

A chorus of cheers from his Warriors went up from the shop above. Oh, shitballs. What had she done? Jett pushed past Inanna, who winked at him, and took the stairs three at a time. He surfaced to the chaos of what happens when Dragon Warriors high on episodes of My Super Sweet 16 meet White Witch influenced party shop attendants at a unicorn disco.

There was even a glittery mirrored ball hanging from the

ceiling, and... was that a unicorn shaped ice-cream machine pooping rainbow sherbet? Yes, yes it was. Jett shook his head. He was so fucked.

"Boss, we hit the mother load. Also, can we bring these very lovely ladies home with us? I'm sure one of them must be my mate. You said we would know when we found her." Several of the men were behind the counter making eyes at the women working to wrap up all the merchandise the warriors had gathered.

There was no missing the tent in this particular Warrior's pants. Sigh. Great. Now he had to explain the difference between finding one's mate and being horny as fuck.

One of the girls giggled and Jett was just about to warn her that she was about to get more than she expected when his phone went off in his pocket indicating a text from Yvaine.

Where are you? Some grumpy German man just called and said they accept your offer. Offer for what? My birthday present?

Finally, some good news. He tapped a message back. *Yes. Stop snooping.*

Yvaine sent back a GIF of a unicorn sticking its tongue out at him. *I'm not snooping and you're no fun.*

Jett chuckled. *I'll show you fun as soon as I get home and it will definitely include tongues sticking out.*

Speaking of tongues. He'd better buy their party supplies and get them to the newly procured castle before any of his Warriors stuck their tongues in places they shouldn't be. Like into the mouths... or other areas of these lovely shop girls. Actually, the girls were not human at all. Wolftresses if his nose was to be believed. Time to go. "Men, if I let you throw Yvaine's party in a real castle with every single one of these seizure inducing decorations can we go now?"

"Fabulous," the biggest and baddest of the group of Warriors singsonged.

Jett slapped his credit card down on the counter, choked at the total, and glared at the Warrior toting the ice-cream machine down the stairs. There was no way to know if they were throwing the best birthday party ever or creating a rainbowpocalypse. The shop girls didn't seem to care that the group of them came and went magically so Jett slipped into an aisle and found a bit of shadow to take him back down to hell and then across the ocean.

If he encountered any demon wyrms on the return trip he'd simply annihilate them with rainbow glitter exploding birthday candles.

DEMON WYRMS MAKE HORRIBLE PARTY GUESTS

Jett guided the Warriors to the Rhineland and again, they didn't encounter any demon wyrms along the way. There was definitely something wrong. He should have asked the White Witch about that. His greatest fear would be putting Yvaine in danger. The Black Dragon was always trying to access mates and the sway they held over dragons souls.

Either the disappearance of the the wyrms mean they were focused on an unknown mate, one yet to find her Dragon or this was a trap. The Black Dragon knew Jett and the way he thought. The asshole probably put together a ploy to make him feel at ease. No demon wyrms, no worries. But that would be exactly the time for the forces of evil to swoop in and kidnap Yvaine. She wasn't like all the other mates. She didn't have his soul shard, because he didn't have one. She wasn't a witch either, and didn't control any elements. The magic in her blood made her a target.

He and his Wyr needed to keep an extra eye out and be

more vigilant than ever. They popped up in the forest around the castle and the stench of wyrms hit him so fast and hard it made his eyes water.

Jett shifted into his dragon form instantly. *Warriors. Join me. I don't know how they found our new home before it's even official, but I will not allow them to taint this first hold we have outside of Hell. We must make this place safe for Yvaine and your future mates.*

His proclamation was met by growls all around. They were not unaccustomed to battle, but Jett had hoped not to make them fight and kill the beasts they had been not that long ago. He could only hope they all understood these wyrms would never be sentient, never be free of the curse of Ereshkigal and the Black Dragon. They were nothing more than mindless drones that wreaked plague upon the world.

Jett could taste their trepidation in the air. *These wyrms are not our brethren. They have been sent to harm us and their havoc will hurt the humans who live here. We are Warriors, and it is our duty to send the demons back to Hell.*

He looked each of his Warrior in the eye to make sure they understood and was ready to send any that weren't prepared for this battle back to the gasthaus or to protect Yvaine. Each and every one of them returned his gaze with a fire behind their eyes. Good. Promotions to the new Elite team all around.

I'll fly over the top of the tower and take out as many as I can. The rest of you, flush them out the front gate. Do not let them get out of the kill zone. You three spread out and surround the castle and catch any stragglers before they can escape back into the shadow. I don't want any survivors to report back to the Black

Dragon that the new Demon Dragon stronghold can be compromised.

Without another word the Warriors did exactly as they were told, no hesitation, no questions asked. Maybe he'd underestimated his Wyr. They were more ready to fight than he'd been when he'd first emerged from Hell and Erishkigal's curse.

Jett took to the sky and used the dark of night to hide himself from the stupid wyrms. He landed on top of the tower and peered down with his dragon sight into the courtyard. There was no ground to be seen, only a black mass of writhing demon dragons flapping their useless wings and nipping at each other.

They reminded him too much of a stockyard where beasts were corralled ready for the slaughter. It was too easy. Someone had lured these demon dragons here and trapped them inside the walls of his new home. Who the fuck would do that?

An enemy who wanted to destroy the Demon Dragon Wyr's home... or a friend helping to rid the world of demon wyrms? Because taking this many wyrms out while they were penned in this way would be like squashing bugs under his shoe. Easy, but messy.

Jett spread his wings wide and dove for the ground. He detected the slightest shimmer of white magic shielding the area all around the courtyard and recognized the spell. Fallyn had used this exact same spell on her little caverns in Hell filled with her hoards of weapons and Christmas ornaments. It was a simple glamour that kept anyone from seeing in her caves. In this case, the spell kept the wyrms from seeing him.

He circled once and then let out a hot burst of flames that

instantly disintegrated a third of the demons right where they stood into piles of ash and oily blotches on the land below. The rest squawked and shot their pitiful spittle of fire in his direction. Since they couldn't see him, their only weapons were completely useless unless they accidentally aimed it just right. None were that lucky and several actually hit other demon wyrms starting their own rounds of infighting. Stupid beasts.

Jett circled again, examining the situation from every angle to see any way this could be a trap for him or his brethren. No matter which way he looked, he was sure the demons had been trapped for him to eviscerate at his leisure. Like a present.

Fucking hell. He hoped this wasn't his birthday present from Yvaine. Had she been conspiring with Fallyn? No. He wouldn't believe that she would purposefully plan the destruction of any beings, even ones as evil as demon wyrms. Yvaine was everything sweet and good in the world.

Jett dove one more time and in a couple of bursts of dragon's flame, he took out the remaining demons leaving a mass of disgusting black goo puddled in the courtyard. He shot one more burst at a window where a shadow caught his eye. They might be more of the little bastards inside.

Hey, boss. Aren't you going to leave any fun for us?

The collective thoughts of the Warriors joined the one who'd sent him the question over their connection. They were worried about him. Cute.

He was happy to be able to spare them this fight. He circled past the buildings checking the interiors with his dragon sight. He didn't smell any more live wryms there. *Brothers. I have eliminated the threat. Join me at the tower and hide yourselves in the darkness. Something mysterious has happened here tonight and you're going to find out what.*

They were ready for anything. Well, maybe not a unicorn birthday party, but anything hell sent their way. Jett kept a close eye out while filling the Warriors in on what had happened. He allowed one of the Warriors to take charge and assign the rest of the team tasks. Jett was pleased to hear the list of to-dos included investigating in both the human realm and the outskirts of Hell that could be reached from their forest.

What about the party, boss?

Right. He considered that for a minute. Having the party here would send a signal to whoever had planted the demon wyrms at his front door that he took care of his business, regardless if that message was to a friend or foe. He could not risk his mate or his Warriors like that. If even a single demon wyrm escaped into the shadow all of hell would know where he intended to live and store his treasures.

He even wondered if he should abandon the castle all together now. Dammit. *We're still going to have the party, I'm just not sure where. We can't put any mates in danger. I'll send in someone to help you figure it all out while I deal with the castle disaster.*

This new threat making the castle useless for the party plus the spending spree at Poof the Party Store meant they had a boatload of party and no plans. Neither the gasthaus or the apartment he and Yvaine shared was a good enough place to have it. Fuck. There went all his good intentions.

He had one more he could call in to help him save this party for Yvaine. Someone who came with her own Dragon

Warrior entourage and would be safe from any plots from Hell. Time to call in the big guns.

Jett sent his Warriors down to make sure all the demon wyrms were gone and start the clean-up. Then he shifted and pulled out his phone. He scrolled through his contacts and dialed the phone. "Ciara?"

A high-pitched squeal followed by a rapid fire of questions came through the phone. Jett held it further away from his head until Ciara quieted down. Then he answered her questions in order. "No, no, still no, yes, I'm not telling you that, she's happy with it, and I need your help. I want to throw a birthday party for Yvaine."

"Oh," Ciara said, and then was actually quiet for a moment. "That's interesting... Yvaine said... never mind. I can help you. When's her birthday?"

"I don't have a date and I don't have a venue. The place I had, well, let's say I've got a bit of a mess to clean up first. I wanted to have it this weekend. Is that doable?" If neither of them knew their actual birth dates, it didn't really matter when they had the party, but with this new mystery, he wanted to have the party sooner rather than later and as far away from the Rhineland as possible. Besides, for some reason, this weekend, this time of year somehow felt right for celebrating his soulmate.

"I'll do it, this weekend works dandy." Ciara giggled and started in with another battery of questions for him.

Jett didn't have to say another word after that, only a few grunts indicating his agreement to Ciara's plans. She was a pro when it came to planning events and also what made mates happy. He'd had more than a little crush on her before he'd met Yvaine and she was really the only human on the planet he trusted at all.

He should have just called her in the first place. Except now he owed her a favor. Hmm. That would need to be reconciled as soon as possible.

"I've got one more favor to ask, and I'm reminding you of the last time I was at your house and you said you owed me." She really didn't owe him anything, but she'd jokingly said she did when he and Yvaine inadvertently got Ciara and Jakob all riled up and randy for each other.

"Uh-oh. That doesn't sound good. Does this involve using our villa for your sexy times again?" Ciara sounded a little too hopeful on that question.

"No. I wonder if you might be able to put some of my Warriors to work. I'm afraid they've been watching a little too much TV and gotten the wrong idea about human culture." Life was not all parties and glitter with battles against evil thrown in just for funsies.

"You want me to teach them how to be human?" It already sounded like she wasn't going to agree.

Jett rubbed the bridge of his nose. "I want you to teach them how to not act like spoiled sixteen-year-old girls at this birthday party."

Ciara laughed so hard she snorted. "I'm going to need reinforcements for that. I know just the over-bearing mother to knock some sense into them. If I can get her to come back from her extended second honeymoon."

"Thank you. I'll send them to you tomorrow." He didn't wait for Ciara to actually agree or for Jakob, who he knew was probably listening in to tell him he couldn't send his Warriors to the Green Wyr's Villa outside Prague. So, he hung up. Shoot. He should have told her this was a secret from Yvaine.

She was smart, she'd figure it out. Probably already had. There was something special about all Wyvern's mates that way. It was like they could read Dragon Warrior's minds.

Jett surveyed the castle grounds and his Warriors doing their best to clean up. He would join them in a minute. As soon as he quit feeling like he'd fucking failed Yvaine as her mate. He didn't have a place for her to live and couldn't even figure out how to throw her a simple birthday party. There was still a tiny part of him that he didn't want to admit to that while he knew they had given their souls to each other, he still didn't have a soul shard to give to her that symbolized his love for her like all the other mates had.

For the first time since they'd been mated, Jett dreaded going home to her. He still would though. He couldn't help it. He would be forever drawn to her, her light, and her love.

Just thinking about her made him miss her. He jumped down off the tower, shifting only his wings to help him land easily and joined the clean-up crew. He might not be able to bring her to their new home tonight. But he would not let the damn Black Dragon play games with his life. Eventually he would defeat the asshole and when he did, this castle would be waiting for them.

After a long night, Jett stepped into the shadow and emerged in their bedroom. It wasn't yet light out and he hoped to find Yvaine asleep in bed. He would really like to wake her up with an orgasm. She wasn't there though.

A sliver of light shined out from under the bathroom door and he smelled the fruity sensuality of her bare skin mixed with the floral scent of her favorite bubble bath.

This life he was trying to build wasn't good enough for her. She was beauty and innocence and everything good in the world. He was covered in demon wyrm guts and the blackness of his own mood.

"What is she doing with a douchepotato like me?" he whispered under his breath. He didn't expect a reply.

"I've asked myself the same question a hundred thousand times or so over the millennia." The First Dragon stepped out of the shadow in the corner of the room. He looked around and flopped down on the bed with one arm behind his head and crossed his feet. "I felt your presence in the shadow, kid. I rarely get involved much anymore, but you are my first born, and we never got a whole lot of time together, so I thought I'd pop in and give you some fatherly advice."

Eye roll.

Jett wanted to hate the First Dragon for abandoning him in hell, for letting him grow up think the soulless Black Dragon had been his father, but honestly, he could use some of that fatherly advice. He didn't have that brother bond relationship with the other Wyverns that he could go to them with his woes. They accepted him and his Wyr, reluctantly, but that was about it.

"I thought I got the ability to travel through the shadow

from my mother." A demon from hell who the First Dragon had used for his own pleasure.

"You do get it from her. Where do you think I learned to use the shadow? That's not exactly Inanna's favorite place to hang out, you know." The First Dragon found Yvaine's bowl of candies on the nightstand and snagged a handful. "She likes you, you know?"

The White Witch? Yeah. No. "I don't know about that."

"I do." The First Dragon grinned and tossed a candy into the air, catching it on the tip of his tongue. "She wouldn't have worked so hard to find your mate for you if she didn't. She started working on Yvaine long before this whole war with Hell thing went all bananas. With the mates for the rest of our children, she just knows, but she had to search for your girl. She kept saying no one was good enough for you."

Jett shook his head. Not that he was ever letting his precious mate go, but he full-well knew she was completely out of his league. "Good enough for me? I think you've got that backwards, old man."

"Nope. Inanna said over and over she couldn't find the one for you. She went through naiads and dryads and witches galore, she even tested out a really hot phoenix, that I personally was rooting for. None of them were good enough." His father snacked on the candy like he wasn't telling a story that changed Jett's life.

He didn't want to ask, he didn't want anything from the White Witch or the First Dragon. He couldn't help it though. "But why? I'm not even hers. I don't really belong to anyone. Except Yvaine."

The First Dragon chuckled. "Yeah. I'm pretty sure your mate would poop glitter all over your head if she thought you didn't belong to her in a deep and meaningful way. You don't want that. I speak from experience."

The First Dragon and the White Witch were sickeningly sweet and devastatingly in love with each other as far as Jett could tell. He sort of assumed they were always a solid team. Except then there was him. A bastard child. Somewhere along the way, their life wasn't perfect. "What kind of experience?"

"A story for another day, lad." He popped another candy into his mouth, sucked on it for a second, made a sour face and spit it out. "Black licorice. Blech. Just know that everyone else around you thinks you're the bomb, so maybe it's time you started thinking you were too."

"Who the fuck cares what anyone else thinks of me?" Except Yvaine. She was the only one whose opinion of him mattered.

"That's my boy." His father rolled up off the bed and slapped Jett on the shoulder. "Now go give 'em hell. Oh, wait. Don't actually give Hell to anyone, that's your inheritance. Forget I said that. How about, umm, I got it. Give her orgasms. Mates like that."

If ever Jett wanted to roll his eyes and groan it was right now. "Thanks."

"Oops. Gotta go. Remember what I said. You're gonna do great, kid." With that last bit of advice, the First Dragon disappeared and left only a sprinkling of rainbow-colored scales in his wake.

"Jett? Is that you? Come join me and I'll give you an early birthday present." Yvaine's voice floated through the room. "And by present, I mean to do naughty things to you I can't say out loud no matter how hard I try."

Yvaine loved him and he would never question that again.

Her opinion was the only one that mattered and tomorrow he would strive again to be the proud Wyvern and the great mate she deserved. Even if that meant finding another god-damned castle for them to live in and throwing her a pink sparkly birthday party every day for the rest of their lives. He would do it for her and he'd do a good fucking job of it too.

He followed his father's advice and he followed it well. Yvaine invented several new words to describe their fuckery fun that morning in the bathtub including flub-dubbery, fluffinstuff, and free-pie-day. That last one was destined to become a long-time favorite of his.

Later he checked in on the birthday team and Ciara. Well, Ciara called Yvaine's cell phone and he answered.

"Ciara. Tell me Yvaine's party is good to go and my Warriors haven't driven you insane." He half expected her to yell at him for sticking her with his party obsessed crew.

"We're all good, except for having a venue. Your boys said something about a castle? Sounds super-sweet-a-riffic for this kind of party to me. Especially if I can get in there a day early to decorate. She's going to lurve the stuff you picked out for the party. I couldn't have done better than if I went to Poof the Party Store myself."

"I'm not sure the castle is safe." But it was good to know he had the pro party planner's approval of the decorations and the theme for the party.

"I have no doubt you can make it safe. Now, put Yvaine on the phone, I have some things to discuss with her too." Ciara always was a demanding woman. Thank goodness she wanted to be friends with Yvaine.

Huh. Did he just get steamrolled by Ciara into keeping that castle? Yes. Yes, he did. Fine. She was right, he couldn't let the forces of Hell dictate where he lived. Either he and his warriors made their home safe or they didn't. He knew more about how demon wyrms, the Black Witch, and the Black Dragon operated than anyone else. If he couldn't secure his home from them, no one could.

"You're sure she'll like it? Maybe a more formal affair with tuxedos and dresses would be better for an event at a castle. Or suits of armor and ballgowns?"

"Jett." Ciara eye-rolled so hard he could hear it in her voice. "I'm sure because she'll love that this is what you wanted to do for her. That matters more than any decorations or party favors. Now, shoo. Yours is not the only party I'm planning at the moment."

Okay then. "Just a second, let me find Yvaine."

She was in the kitchen making a cake. "Ack. You're not supposed to see this. Go away."

Jett handed her the phone, gave her a little kiss on the cheek, and swiped his finger through the dark frosting. Mmm, chocolate. "I didn't see a thing. I've got to check on our new house, but don't make any plans for tomorrow, okay?"

"Crudmuffins. I already... never mind. Okay." She smiled at him so brightly, he needed sunglasses. "See you later, you shmexy beast."

Yvaine shoved him toward the front door, out into the hall, and shut the door behind him. He chuckled when he heard her squeal at whatever she and Ciara were talking about. She was definitely having more fun planning his birthday than he was hers.

He stepped into the shadow and headed for the castle. This time he decided to spend a little time in the dark to investigate the area around their new home. All was as he expected.

Several rich veins of gold that would help fund the Wyr for years to come, a good number of underground caverns he could use for his treasure hoard, and no signs of demon wyrms at all.

Hopefully the elements had helped clean up the mess in the courtyard. The ashy remains of the wyrms should blow away easily, but he would probably have to get a cleaning crew in to scrub the black oily stains from the cobblestones. He appeared out of the shadow and into the courtyard right near his own front door.

Hanging from the doorknocker was a glass ornament in the shape of a dragon that had a note hanging from its neck with his name scrawled across the front. It sparkled and gleamed, even though there wasn't any light shining on it. Jett gently lifted the ornament off and opened the note.

~Hope you enjoyed my gift. I know your unicorn wouldn't have liked to be taken by the wyrms so I brought them to you instead.

"Fallyn," he growled and looked around the courtyard and into the windows of the house. He didn't sense her presence or see any other signs of her simple spells. She had brought the demon wyrms. But why? Everything Fallyn did was a mystery, but she always had a purpose. She was a crafty one.

Jett spent most of the day searching every nook and cranny of the castle to make sure it was secure and wyrm free. There were some interesting relics hidden in the oldest parts of the structure, but no evil. He used his own power over the shadow to create a maze of misdirection for anyone trying to use it to travel to the castle or the surrounding forest, save for the one spot where he'd appeared in the courtyard. That way if any uninvited guests did decide to show up for the party, they would be instantly under the eye of everyone there.

When he was satisfied that he'd done all he could to make the castle the safest place he could for his Wyr and his mate, he shifted and called to all of his brethren to invite them home. Pride coursed through his veins like the hottest fire and the strongest shadow. The only time he'd ever felt prouder than today was when he and Yvaine and declared their love for each other and she'd agreed to be his.

Some of his Demon Dragon Warriors appeared out of the shadow in the courtyard right away and he welcomed each and every one. More would arrive over the coming days. Just in time for Yvaine's party. He encouraged them to explore their new home and claim spaces of their own. Some would choose rooms, but he knew most would prefer to remain outside where they felt free to come and go. That had become an important part of their freedom for many of his Warriors, and a big reason why he'd like this particular property in the first place.

One of the Warriors from the party crew popped in. "Ready for us to come in and decorate, boss?"

"I am. I'm looking forward to showing off your efforts to Yvaine this weekend." He patted the Warrior on the back.

The man straightened up to his full height and his fire glowed in his eyes. "Thank you, sir. We won't let you down."

No. They wouldn't. Jett had no doubt this party would be, as Yvaine might say, supercaliunicornicallyexpidocispectacular.

SURPRISE

The evening of Yvaine's party bloomed with a brilliant full moon. Several times Yvaine came into his office, stared at him like she was going to say something and then would turn and run out. She'd been fidgety and nervous most of the day, but he couldn't figure out why. Probably because she hated keeping secrets and this had something to do with his birthday party. He hadn't told her that her party was tonight. He wanted her to be surprised and he didn't mind keeping those kinds of secrets from her.

This last time, she came in, he grabbed her and pulled her onto his lap. The party would be ready to start, and not only would his Demon Dragons be arriving, but so would the Wyverns of the other Wyrs. Ciara assured him they would want to be there. "Sweetheart. How would you like to go see our new home with me?"

Her eyes went wide. "The castle?"

"Yes. I'd like to show it to you, make sure it's a place you'll want to call home. There is a nice big forest all around for you to run free in. He knew she was going to love it, but he couldn't help but worry just a little since he hadn't actually shown it to her before buying it.

He had to trust his gut because his gut was always right when it came to Yvaine. He should have learned to trust it a lot sooner.

She wiggled like a little kid waiting to open a present. "Like you want to go right now?"

He tipped his head at her and frowned. "Unless you have somewhere else you need to be."

She grabbed his face and planted a big old kiss on his lips. "Mmm-mmm. Yes. Let's go. Right now. Yay!"

"You're being weird." Secrets did not agree with her. He should have let her make his birthday a week ago like she wanted to. He'd remember that for future birthdays.

She jumped up. "Am not. Come on. Let's go. No, wait. Let me get something first."

Yvaine sprinted into their bedroom and came back with a box wrapped in brown paper under her arm. "Now I'm ready. Shadow or flying?"

He eyed the box. Maybe something she'd bought for the new house. "Whichever you prefer. It's not far, so we can fly if you prefer."

"Yeah. I don't want to hurl my cookies. They were too delicious to waste that way." She licked her lips and he almost called the party off to take advantage of that tongue.

He led her out to the rooftop of their little apartment building and shifted into his dragon form. Yvaine crawled into one of his big claws and wrapped one arm around her box and the other around his leg. "Ready or not, here we come."

Jett took to the sky and headed toward the Rhineland. He used small shadows created by the clouds and the moon to keep them hidden from prying human eyes. It didn't take more than a few minutes until the rivers and forests around their new home came into view.

The tower of the castle was lit up with pink searchlights and the disco ball was in full swing, sending lights and sparkles all across the tower's stone walls and into the courtyard. Cripes. Not like he could keep that a surprise.

He kept quiet until they landed in the courtyard that was filled with more dragons and people than he thought it could even hold. Jett shifted right away and pulled Yvaine into his arms.

"Surprise," he said.

"Surprise," Yvaine said at the same time. Then she giggled. "Why did you say surprise? This is your birthday party."

Jett looked around and all the decorations he and the Warriors had picked out were scattered all throughout the courtyard, but for every unicorn there was also a dragon. There were even two cakes in the center on a table as big as a truck. One pink and laden with glittering sugar sprinkles and one dark chocolate. His favorite.

He lifted Yvaine up and spun her around. "Look around, love. This is your birthday party too."

They both searched out Ciara and found her grinning like a dragon who'd just uncovered a whole new hoard of gold. "Surprise. It's awfully cute that the two of you chose Valentine's Day to celebrate each other's birthdays."

"Who are Val and Tine?" Yvaine asked. "Why do they get a whole day named after them? I declare today Jett and Yvaine's day. That has a way better ring to it."

Ciara smiled and looked to Jett to explain. He shrugged. He didn't know who Val or Tine were either. Ciara's mouth dropped open. "Seriously? I'm going to have to put you two through pop culture one-oh-one. Valentine's Day is the holiday for celebrating love."

Yvaine frowned. "I don't need a day for that. I love Jett every day. Val and Tine are dumb."

Ciara waved Yvaine over and whispered in her ear, then she whipped out her cell phone and showed something to Yvaine. Jett couldn't see or hear, but he did catch the way Yvaine's eyes glittered and her frown turned into a very naughty smile. He had no idea what Ciara was showing Yvaine, but he had a feeling he was going to have to thank her later.

Yvaine laughed her ass off and waggled her eyebrows at him. "Val and Tine are not as dumb as I thought they were."

She dragged Jett onto the dance floor. "Ciara showed me a part of movie that I assume Val and Tine were the stars of, and said I should make you dance dirty with me for my birthday because it would make you want to do the horizontal dirty dancing with me later."

Dancing was not in his skill set. Only for Yvaine would he make a fool out of himself.

"Oh, I almost forgot to give you your birthday present." She dragged him back off the dance floor and over to the box she'd brought with her. "Open it, open it, open, open, open."

Jett tore the paper just to make her smile. He tossed the lid of the box off and stared at the contents. Inside were a handful of t-shirts, every single one with a unicorn printed on it with a completely inappropriate saying.

The first read: *I'd Rather Be Riding My Unicorn.*

"Ha. Get it. I"m your unicorn and that's a naughty innuendo." Yvaine clapped her hands and pulled the shirt out to reveal the next one.

Shirt number two read: *Just The Tip.*

There were even more underneath that one.

Unicorns Make Me Horny

Bitch, Please. I Ride A Unicorn.

Sorry, I Can't. I Have To Ride My Unicorn

And the last one that had a dragon on it instead of a unicorn. The dragon had smears of rainbow all around its mouth and this shirt read: *I Ate The Last Unicorn.*

Dear Goddess, he'd created a monster.

Yvaine pulled the last shirt out of the box and made him put it on. Then she pulled off the plain pink sweatshirt she'd been wearing to reveal a t-shirt with a unicorn on a stripper pole that read: *My Husband Rides A Unicorn.*

"I made them for you. Do you like your presents?"

What? Like he was going to say no? Of course not. He was going to wear her slightly naughty t-shirts every day for the rest of his life. "I love them. Now it's my turn to give you a present."

He wasn't as creative as she was and didn't have much he could give her anyway. The only thing important that he had to give was himself. He couldn't give her a piece of his soul because she already had all of it as far as he was concerned. "I made you something too."

Jett pulled a small velvet jewelry box out of his pocket and presented it to her. "Ooh. Is it the keys to our new castle?"

All of a sudden, he was slightly nervous the home-made

gift wasn't good enough. His gut slapped him upside the head for even thinking that. "Open it."

She lifted the lid of the long box and gasped. Inside was a necklace with a charm on the end of a chain. He lifted it out of the box and dangled it so she could see it before he placed it around her neck. He'd fashioned the charm out of shadow into the shape of a heart that beat and pulsed in time to his own. He'd put his heart and soul into making this gift fo her. "It's my heart and it's yours. Always and forever."

The soft voice of the Goddess whispered in his mind. *I knew she was the right one to show you the light inside your own heart. Break the final hold of Erishkigal's curse. Let Yvaine and all your brethren see what true love is.*

Warmth spread across his chest and radiated out. The part of his soul that had long been hidden, the piece he'd kept buried deep so that no one could ever hurt him with it, burst out of the darkness. Black light glowed right through his skin and his new t-shirt, brighter than any Dragon Warrior's soul shard ever had.

The light reflected in Yvaine's eyes and blinked back the tears that bubbled up along her lashes. She pressed her hand to his chest and the light danced across her skin. "Jett. It's the most beautiful thing I've ever seen. I love it more than you could ever know."

"I know." Jett knew better than anyone else in heaven or hell exactly what it meant to have the true love of the one and only true mate for him. The true love of his unicorn.

The black light shot out from between Yvaine's fingers and the necklace at her throat simultaneously, like a thousand fireworks. It crackled through the night like electricity and struck each and every Demon Dragon Warrior directly in the chest. They didn't appear hurt, but all the members of his Wyr did look stunned. The light glowed in their chests and one by one, an amulet made of shadow and a piece of their souls appeared on a cord hanging around their necks.

Soul shards. The Demon Dragons had the missing piece they needed to find their own soul mates.

The First Dragon flew across the sky above their heads, doing several loopty-loops. He shot multi-colored flames that dissipated into smoke that formed a sparkling design in the sky. Jett shook his head staring up into sky at the giant heart and some kind of weird baby shooting an arrow through it.

"There goes the neighborhood. Just what I need, more dragons who want mates to give their dark souls to." Fallyn stepped out of the shadow at Yvaine's side. She wrinkled her nose and squeezed one eye shut like someone speared her in the head with a hot poker. "Shh, witches. I'll get to you."

Yvaine grabbed Fallyn into a big hug and held her tight. Fallyn closed her eyes and leaned against Yvaine's shoulder like she was exhausted. For one whole second the strange girl Jett had never called sister, but probably should have, looked vulnerable, scared, and like she needed something he could never give her.

"You'd better tell them to keep their pants on, Prince. I don't have time to --" Fallyn's eyes darted from side to side seeing something only in her mind. She shut her lids for a moment, sucked in a deep breath, and when she opened her eyes again, the old badass Fallyn looked back at them again. "Dammit. Not yet."

Fallyn disappeared back into the shadow, but Jett caught a glimpse of a reflection, like a mirror, and then she was gone.

Yvaine grabbed Jett's hand and squeezed it tight. "We have to help her, you know?"

Jett wished he knew how. It was so very sweet of his mate. She wanted to bring everyone into their strange and cobbled together version of a family. He loved her all the more for it. "Fallyn can take care of herself."

"Hmm." Yvaine laid her head on his shoulder. "She's definitely a badass, but I wish she had someone like I have you."

If Jett with his dark, broken soul could find a mate so incredibly special and perfect for him, maybe there was someone for Fallyn too. "If anyone can figure out how to help her find her mate, love, it's you. But not tonight. It's your birthday and I'm not letting anything or anyone interfere with this celebration."

Yvaine got the cutest of naughty grins on her lips. "You want to celebrate, do you?"

Whatever she had in mind, he was one-hundred percent up for. Jett pulled Yvaine into the center of the courtyard where shimmering rainbow glitter from the First Dragon's scales twinkled in the air along with the light from the disco ball. "I do, but first let's try your dirty dancing."

A song about a little cafe just the other side of the border. Yvaine was giving him looks that made his mouth water.

"Come a little bit closer, you're my kind of dragon. So big and so strong." Yvaine giggled and the love glowed not just in her eyes, but in the new amulet she wore around her throat.

He wrapped one arm around her lower back, took one hand, and pulled her tight to his chest. Together they swayed to the beat of the music, their hips pressed together, their eyes locked. Their bodies moved together so perfectly, in such a sensual rhythm, it was almost as good as sex. Almost.

Yvaine brushed her lips over his an snuck her tongue into his mouth. He deepened the kiss until they were both ready to tear each other's clothes off.

"Get a room, you two." Ciara shouted from somewhere behind him.

That was a very good idea. Luckily, he had a good dozen or so rooms in his possession already. Jett grabbed Yvaine around the backs of her thighs and wrapped her legs around his waist. Without a word to the rest of the guests, who were hooting and hollering, he took his mate into the castle.

A trail of paper heart confetti led to the last bedroom along one of the hallways. Inside, the room was furnished simply with a big bed, a few candles, and a soft area rug. He'd have to thank Ciara and the Super Sweet crew later for thinking of everything he could ever possibly want for his birthday.

Yvaine yanked his new t-shirt over his head and ran her hands across his bare skin. "This is the best birthday ever."

Jett wasn't going to disagree with that. He pressed her back into the soft blankets, and pushed her greedy hands over her head. "I'm going to make it even better for you right now."

He scraped his teeth across the shadowy red and black mark of the dragon on her neck. Yvaine groaned and squirmed beneath him. He would ride his unicorn until those little moans turned into cries of pleasure. Then she'd ride her Dragon into the night.

Their love and magic danced and bringing them closer together with every touch and kiss. No force could ever break the bond between them. No evil, no dark magic, no curse. Because their love could conquer all.

BE sure to read the next book in the Dragons Love Curves series - *Dirty Dragon.*

Available on Amazon and free as part of Kindle Unlimited

DRAGON LOVE LETTERS

DEAR READER

*D*ear Reader,

There's nothing more fun than a beautiful love letter. Except maybe a juicy one.

Here in this special collection of fun-sized stories, I've collected something special for you. Love letters from Dragons.

Our favorite Dragon Warriors have written personal notes to their lady loves.

Why?

Now is the time before the finale book in the Dragons Love Curves series, telling the tales of the Dragon Warriors and the sassy, curvy women that they love as they battle the Black Dragon and Ereshkigal, the dark witch and queen of hell.

The Dragons know that an epic battle between good and evil is coming, as it has been foretold in *Dirty Dragon* and *Crave Me.* Some of them have written letters for their mate in case they die, some to make sure their mates know how much they love them, and another still in a desperate hour of needing her above all others.

We don't often get to see the softer side of our badass alpha warriors so enjoy their mushy gushy, lovey dovey, and sometimes corny about love letters.

Extra thanks to Tracey A. and Franciszka G. for just in time proofreading the letters for me (except Match's! That one's been a tightly guarded secret!). Any remaining mistakes are mine alone.

Before you turn the page to read the love letters, I want to give a shout out to the amazing women in my Facebook Group - Aidy's Amazeballs. We worked on some of these letters together and it was some of the funnest writing times of my life. Love you ladies!

XOXO
    --Aidy

DEAR INANNA

*D*earest luscious mate of mine Inanna, the White Witch,

My Dragon sons have learned from the very smart women in their lives about a fantastical holiday called Valentine's Day. I believe you would approve of the sentiment as it involves chocolate and sex (and occasionally massacres. Delightful, isn't it?)

Oh, they also tell me that to show my love for you, I should write an ooey-gooey letter. Instead I will write one on paper with a pen as I feel writing on a cinnamon roll with icing would be much harder.

How does one write a love letter to a Goddess? Especially when she is both the Goddess of love and war? I cannot tell you how beautiful your body is to me, because I'm sure you already know since I praise your curves and eyes and thighs each and every day.

Shall I tell you how I adore your sneaky and crafty brain? This you also know since you are far smarter than I and come up with the most brilliant intrigues to foil our enemies.

Maybe I should sing a song of how my heart and soul sing at the way you care so much for every single one of our children, the way you battle for their happiness. Alas, of course you know, as I campaign for the same by your side.

Instead I shall tell you that each and every time one of our sons finds his true mate (mostly because you and I shove them headfirst toward the right boy or girl) my own soul reignites for you just as it did the day we first met.

I know exactly what my boys are feeling as they touch the one woman who fulfills their soul. When I touched you, I forgot. I wanted to throw flames of fire through the air to announce my need, but I couldn't even take a breath. I called upon the earth to bring you all the flowers of the world, the water to provide you refreshment, and the wind to cool your skin.

Yet you did not see me. You did not feel the lust, need, and pure unfettered emotion. My spirit sank into the darkest depths of Hell and I swore to shield my broken, chained heart from feeling anymore for all time.

It wasn't until, on the verge of defeat, I pulled my powers in and my heart shined with the power of a thousand stars. You saw how my soul burned for yours and we both knew our love was meant to be.

Someday we should tell that story to our progeny. They should know how clever you are to pull those glowing shards of their own souls from their hearts so they too can follow the light to find their true mates. Ah, someday... when our war with the dark forces of the underworld is won.

Until then I will continue to burn for you, because it is our deep magical love that gives me strength for each and every battle. I need no holiday or angel cupid baby with a bow to shoot an arrow at my ass on a candy-coated holiday to tell you or show you all my mushy gushy feelings for you.

I wish for you and me to spend all the rest of eternity wrapped up in each other's body, where I can lick you and claim you and make you mine over and over. Your orgasms will be many as you claim me and make me yours in return. Hmm. That sounds like the perfect Valentine's Day celebration.

Unless of course you'd rather fight off a horde of demon wyrms with me. Also fun.

Nah. Let's do the schmexy times instead.

With all my mushiest of kisses,

-- Kur, The First Dragon

P.S.

Quit telling our Dragon Warrior Sons they are your favorite douchepotatoes. You know I'm your favorite of all.

*wink

DEAR CIARA

*M*y Ciara,

Thief of my heart. What in the hell I did to deserve you as a mate, I don't know. Every time I see you, after I catch my breath again, I thank the First Dragon and the White Witch for all of their matchmaking shenanigans.

Even that first time I saw you, when I thought you were my enemy, a witch out to harm me and my brethren, my soul knew better.

Before I saw you for the first time, your scent drew me across the ocean to find you. No other woman has ever smelled so sweet. Like fresh rain on the grass, the sweetest ripe berries, freshly tilled earth, and everything green. I should have known then you were no enemy of mine.

Did you know that after I landed on that balcony, I watched you sitting in that fancy ballroom, taking those slow sensual bites of that cake? I wanted to be that fork, be the sugar that made you moan in pleasure. My body warred with my mind. I had every intention of finding some demon thief and tearing it to shreds for stealing the First Dragon's relic.

Instead I found you and your sassy mouth, your curves that go on for miles, and the beautiful power inside of you just waiting to come out and wreck my life in all the best ways.

I did everything I could to intimidate you, but no... you went toe-to-toe with me, not backing down for a minute. All I wanted in that moment was to take you and shake you, because it was either that or kiss you until we were both senseless.

Every part of my soul screamed for me to mark you, claim you, mate you, make you mine.

I thought you'd cast a spell on me. Everyone knew Dragon Warriors didn't have mates anymore. There was no way in hell you could be mine. No Dragon had found their true mate in almost a century. We were doomed.

Then you came along and rocked my fucking world.

You changed everything.

How could I not kidnap you and take you away? I wanted to hide you away from the world in my hoard forever, only mine. I didn't care how the other Wyverns would react, I didn't care if you were working with the demon wyrms. I only cared that you made me feel something I never thought I would.

Love.

It couldn't be. Yet it was.

I was the only Dragon in the world to be blessed with a soul mate. A beautiful human woman, who didn't know her own power or worth, but that was stronger and more important to the fate of the world than she could ever know.

I try every day to be worthy of you and your feisty, perfect soul.

I wanted to put these words down in a permanent form

now because I fear a great battle is coming. How I wish I could protect you from the evil hunting us. I'd wrap you up in my wings and kiss you until the war with hell is over and done.

It pains my heart that we can't. I know the White Witch has chosen you to help save Dragonkind because you are so very special. We can't defeat the minions of hell without your powerful gifts. I will stand by your side, hand in hand, as we fight for all that is good in this world. My heart will shutter at every turn, but I will stand strong for you.

Our love is what will conquer the darkness.

Until then, stay safe in my arms as I am in your heart.

Yours always,

Jakob

DEAR FLEUR

*M*y Dearest lush flower,

I do not fear death. I have tasted the afterlife and know that the First Dragon and the White Witch await me with the just rewards for a warrior's proud death in this battle of good and evil. I do not fear the Black Dragon and his foul attempts to take what rightfully belongs to a Dragon Warrior. I do not fear the machinations of Ereshkigal and her army of demon wyrms wreaking havoc on our world.

No, I do not fear the dark. Not since you became the light in my life.

The final battle is coming, I feel it in my soul. What role you and I must play in this fight, I'm not sure. But it will be an important one if the gifts given to you by the First Dragon and the White Witch are any indication. While I am not afraid of my own death, I cannot hide from you the worry I bear for your own beautiful life.

Or what it would mean to me to lose you.

If I could choose to live any day over again, it would be the day we first met. You in that pretty pink top and tight jeans with just the barest sliver of skin showing drove me insane from the first moment I laid eyes on you. I wanted you so badly and you thought I was just some lothario stripper dude.

Magic Mike's got nothing on me, baby.

I wish I could say that I won you over and made you fall in love with me in an instant. But you were too smart for that. Thank goodness the First Dragon and the White Witch helped me out or I might still be begging you on hands and knees to be my mate.

My life, my soul has never been the same and I'm so grateful. Even when the darkest hours are upon us, I wouldn't change a thing. Not even when you made me sleep in the bathtub. I've developed a special fondness for daisies and while I wouldn't ever admit it to anyone else but you, I can't help but get hard as rock whenever I see one.

My desire for you grows like the blooming flowers as if every day was the beginnings of spring. I love you more each and every day and a love like ours can never die. No matter what happens, no matter the trials and tribulations ahead, I want... no need you to know that I love you and everything about our life together.

You must promise me this. Should I fall in battle, and even your healing power cannot save me, you mustn't pine over my grave as your mother has. You must fight to live a full and beautiful life. You deserve as much. Know that I will be watching over you from the afterlife.

Although... I can't promise I won't come back and kick any dragon's ass who thinks he can become your new mate.

You are mine forever and ever, in this life and the next.
With all my love,
--Steele

DEAR JADA

*E*taku ipo,

Of all the mates in the wide *taiao,* there will never be another for me, only you. You're my bright star on the horizon of the deep blue sea, guiding my heart and soul. I will be ever grateful you came into my life.

For so long I thought I would live a dog's life, never truly caring about anything or anyone but myself. I did my duty to my people, for the Wyr, but my existence was a half life, self-ishly lived. Yet, I didn't even realize the truth of that. Until you.

You changed me, changed my life, and I thank the First Dragon and the White Witch for their brilliant meddling each and every time I lay my eyes on you. I can hardly wait to see how our future together unfolds. I want a dozen dragon sons to teach the ways of my Maori ancestors, show them to swim and play in the blue waters of the ocean, and watch them with pride as they take their own places among the Dragon Warriors.

But for every son, I also want a daughter, with the chubbiest of cheeks, the rosiest of smiles, and the most beautiful of hearts, just like yours.

Imagine our happy family, the boys terrorizing the waves, and the girls terrorizing the boys, as we watch over them and grow into our Wisdom together, loving, laughing, and loving some more.

I don't know if that's what lies ahead for us. I can only dream and pray to our *atua*, The First Dragon, to convince the fates who showed me the way to you that we would live a good life if they should grant it. But I must also pray to *Tū-whakamoana-ariki*, to give me and my Blue Dragon Warriors everything we need to defeat the forces of evil that plague the world.

Our adventures together have shown me that it will take more than what I and the other Dragon Wyverns and our Warriors can do on our own to restore balance between good and evil. I wish I could shelter you from the terrible tempest, but without you and all of the precious mates, I don't think we can win.

Each and every day I watch you grow more skillful in your own right, using the gift of the shadow and your irresistible allure. How I ever believed you wielded your powers for anything but the good is a guilt I will forever bear. But it is a burden I happily hold in my soul because it also means I found you.

I can find anything in the world. You're the only thing I ever needed to find.

Should the battle ahead open the *tatau o te pō* and I'm taken back to *Rarohenga*, know that my heart and soul will not go too. They will remain safe in your embrace until we can be together in this life or the next. Knowing you hold the most important parts of me to your breast is what lends me the strength to give my all to the coming battle.

I am ever yours and forever grateful that you are mine. I strive every day to make sure you know how much I love you but in case I have ever failed I'll say it here again so you will never doubt how deep my feelings run for you.

Ka nui taku aroha ki a koe.

I love you.

Aroha nui,

--Ky

DEAR AZY

*L*ight of my soul,

So much has changed in our lives in the short time we've been together. I feel I've known you my entire life. But you weren't even a twinkle in your mother's eye when I was born. I'm not even sure what mermaid lifespans are like, your mother may not have been around when I was a child.

How the universe, the First Dragon, and the White Witch had to conspire to bring us together boggles my mind. My life would have been so frivolous without you and our babes.

I have gladly waited almost two-hundred years for you, fought through heaven and hell to find you, and given up my soul, more than once... for you.

To think that our time together could be cut short -- No. I cannot. I will do everything in my power and maybe beyond to live a long and loving life by your side, as we watch our children grow, find their own mates, and have grandbaby dragons of their own.

I would do anything to protect you, Apollo and Isolde,

even if that means a sacrifice I don't want to make. All of Dragonkind is counting on me to lead them into a final battle between us and the forces of Hell.

Am I a strong enough warrior to do both that and hold on to you and our family?

I pray to the First Dragon that it is so. If anyone has given me the strength it is you, my beautiful badass mate. I'll never understand how I was blessed to have you as my true fated mate.

I live for the day I can return the mantle of AllWyvern, alpha of the Dragon Warriors back over to Match. Then you and I will take a long vacation where we can lie around in the sun, splash in the ocean, and I can give you more orgasms than you can count.

We'll make more babies, a dozen at least, and I'll teach them to fly and you'll teach them to swim and we'll keep them young for an extra hundred years just for the fun of it.

I could spend all my days and nights dreaming of our ideal life together, but I must not. I fear I have turned into the worst kind of worrier, one that cannot plan for every contingency, for every battle, for all the losses yet to come.

I want you to know that no matter what happens in the coming dark days, my heart and soul belongs to you forever and always. Without you, I was close to death and your grace, tenacity, kind heart, and dirty mouth saved me from a fate worse than death. I am better because of you and would never have been able to live up to my full potential as alpha without knowing you were by my side.

You were the miracle I needed, and you blessed me with more than a miracle when we had the twins. I send all my hopes, dreams and wishes that you will never need to read this letter, because I get to show you each and every day how much I love you, need you, and cherish you.

Should the worst happen, and I cannot be by your side, you must trust that my heart and soul are always yours. I love you more than I ever imagined was possible. Even the forces of evil, death itself can never change that.

Our love story isn't over, it's a journey of a thousand lifetimes, unending.

 Unendingly yours,

--Cage

DEAR YVAINE

*M*y dearest Yvaine,
      I may not be a poet, I'm rarely very good with words. I fear I haven't told you often enough how I truly feel. I hope that my actions and the way I downright need you, is proof enough that I love you so deeply that my life would be nothing without you.

Before the first time you walked out of the dark and into my world, I thought my life had a purpose, a dark and dangerous self-serving purpose. How wrong I was. Vengeance controlled my lost soul then and had no idea how your love would change me and show me my true path in this world.

The shadows have shown me, whispered in my mind, and awakened me in the midst of my sleep to make sure I know, a final battle with the forces of evil are coming. Our Black Demon Dragon Warriors and I must fight Kur-Jara and Ereshkigal to the end... either theirs or ours. They are a plague on our world, a curse to all, and they must be stopped.

It breaks my newly found heart that I could ever leave you. I don't want to. If I could I would wrap us both up in the soft feather bed you chose for us and kiss you senseless for hours. I would make sure you had so many orgasms that you'd swear you had no more to give me. You'd beg me with all your favorite swear words like flark, flagenstuben, and fluffernutter. While we both laugh, we'd make love until the end of time.

Alas, I fear that you above all others would not allow me to shield us from the dark times ahead. I have never known bravery as strong as yours and even knowing these could be our last days together, you would still push me to fight for the freedom of my brethren. Freedom for all of Dragonkind from the machinations of the underworld.

Because we both know that what we're truly defending is our newly found family, our future, and our ability to love each other.

Since I know I'm not good at telling you how I feel, and maybe I haven't done the best job of showing you, I want to make sure you know exactly what's in my heart and soul before it's too late.

Love of my life, light of my soul, you above all others know that I never thought anyone as pure of heart and as special as you would ever come into my life. I never thought I could be happy at all, and you've made me a downright smiling fool with all your feelings and mushy kisses.

I will be ever grateful for each and every one of those.

If I should die in this final battle between good and evil, I want you to know above all else that I love you.

I.

Love.

You.

Yvaine.

Nothing will ever take that away from us, nothing will ever change it. I love you with all of my heart and soul, and I will go on loving you until the end of time.

You already had my soul before we ever met, you have my heart always.

Now and forever yours,

—Jett

DEAR JULES

*L*ight of my life,

I still can't believe that I have found love, the missing part of my soul, a mate. Each and every day I feel that the First Dragon and the White Witch are smiling down on me. I imagine they're sending me a little bit of extra luck because I am definitely the luckiest damn Dragon Warrior to have fallen in love with you.

I have this fire in my gut that burns bright with the heat of your love, your power over the sun. Do you know what that fire tells me?

That no matter what lies ahead - and I know that you've seen a vision of our future - because of the strong bonds that Dragon Warriors have forged with our amazeballs mates, love will conquer all.

I know, I know, I'm a total cornball. But I can't help it. There is no way in heaven or hell I could ever believe anything else. Not after knowing you exist in this world and that you and I belong to each other.

You feed my soul with the light in yours, your conviction

of all things right and just, and your gorgeous fucking curves. I long and lust for you each and every day. You are my sunshine, my only sunshine. But you're even more than that. You're my everything.

You're the fire, the sun, the wind, the will to be the best warrior I can be. How could I not know deep in my heart that the good guys aren't going to win?

We are. We will defeat the Black Dragon and his evil minions. We will send the Black Witch back to the underworld where she can rot in Hell for the rest of eternity. We will win.

And when we have fought the final battle, when we have defeated the forces of Hell, you and I can spend our days lounging naked in the sun, making love, and if I'm very, very lucky, making babies too. I can hardly wait to cup your belly, full and round with our child, in my hands.

We will make gorgeous little Dragon Warrior sons and stunning little witchling daughters. We will teach them to use their powers for good and tell the story of how we fell in love trying to save the wolf pup twins. We will laugh and laugh and love and love.

That is the future I see for us, and nothing will stand in my way of defeating the evil forces trying to bring the world into darkness. With you and the other Dragon Warriors and their mates by our sides, victory is but a battle away. I hold no fear in my heart, only your love, and nothing is stronger than that.

I know there will be sacrifices and some sorrow ahead. I may be a cornball, but I'm no fool. Life isn't perfect and with wins there must also be losses. I only hope that I can be the leader for our Wyr that Match has put faith in me to be. I lead by his example and put my mate and our love above all else.

Together we will be the strength and the shining example of what true love can do, what it can be for all Dragon Warriors.

Thank you for being you, the tough, sassy, savvy, lusciously curvy mate I never knew I needed, and yet now could never live without. In case I haven't told you enough times today (although, I think I'm up to ten or twelve this morning), I love you, dear mate, with all my heart and soul. There will never be another for me. I've been blinded to all others by the light of your love for me.

May our love burn as hot as a thousand suns forevermore.

Love,

--Dax

DEAR PORTIA

*O*ur light in the darkness,

When we were young dragons, not yet warriors, the two of us would fight over every little thing. Who was the fastest flyer, who had the biggest wings, which of us could find more gold and hide it from the other, who would have the most beautiful and fiercest mate when we grew up.

Once we received our shared soul shards, and worked to become the best Dragon Warriors in our Wyr, we watched our greatest friend become our Wyvern and shared an intense gratitude to have a brother by our side as Cage bestow on us the highest of honors of Second and Master at Arms of the Gold Dragon Wyr.

While we competed to be the best, it was always fun and games, because we each wanted the best for the other. That's what being born cursed twins meant. We grew in time to understand that a mate was never a part of our fate. Even when the other Dragon Warriors were blessed with their heart's own match, we were resigned to being the best, minus the best part of our own damned soul.

Then we met you.

Gris ~

My love,

I wanted so much to hate you. I understood my fate, knew my path, and was ready and willing to bear the burdens of life as only the Second Wyvern of the powerful Gold Dragon Wyr. I was absolutely sure that was all I needed in my life.

You made me see how wrong I was, and I love you so for being you, being the mate of my soul.

Sun above, those first days of wanting and needing you, but forcing myself to hide my true feelings, even from myself were pure torture. How could you do this to me? Upend everything I knew to be true with a sensual look, a sashay of your hips, and the way you were so scared of me yet refused to back down.

I curse the day I denied the light of my soul shard. Fate practically shoved you right in front of me and I was dumb enough to think I knew better. Thankfully my body knew better. It took losing you for my head to catch up to my heart.

These days with you to warm my bed and my soul, my greatest fear is that I don't tell you enough how much I love you.

I love you, Portia, no matter what, forever and ever. Each day as the sun rises, and again when it sets, I thank the First Dragon and the White Witch for knowing you were the one we needed to make us complete. I hold sacred in my soul the day three became one.

Zon ~

Love of mine,

How could I not give you my heart and my soul? I was a fool for ever thinking they were mine to begin with. Every bit of my heart, every part of my soul was always yours.

Every day since we first met, I strive to be the Warrior you need and deserve in your life. I know I'm not always good with words, but I hope I show you through my actions and my body how much I love you.

I can't imagine my life without you and Gris in it. Together, we three broke a centuries old curse with nothing more than the purest part of ourselves. Love.

I never knew a battle could be won by that sacred element. I've always used swords, brawn, prowess, and my Dragon Warrior gifts to defeat my foes. I don't think any of the sons of Kur thought that we could be our best, truest selves by sacrificing that armor we wear called loneliness. You tore mine from me the moment we met, and I am forever grateful to have you by my side in life, love, and whatever else fate has in store for us.

IN THE COMING DAYS, the forces of evil will vie for dominance. The Black Dragon and his dark witch will do everything in their power to destroy us. Together, we put our faith in you, love. Not to keep us alive or from harm, that is a part of being a Dragon Warrior. No, we have the utmost faith that no matter what happens, good or bad, that you will keep our souls and our love in your heart.

Knowing that you love us, and that our love for you can never die, never be beaten out of us, never be defeated - that's what will win this war.

Love conquers all.

We are yours and grateful you are ours.

Always,

--Gris

--Zon

DEAR FALLYN

*M*y fires,

     From the first moment I saw you - when we were so young and naive - I knew you were mine. I knew I wanted nothing more than to belong to you.

Together we would change the world.

The world changed. But it wasn't because of our love.

Now, in these dark and dangerous times, you have nothing but hatred and fear in the depths of your soul for me.

My heart is broken. Broken for you, and all that you have suffered. Broken for me and everything we have lost, everything we have never had together.

I never wept. I never moaned for you in the night. Never once did I let the loss of you and the beauty our love could have been make me weak. I could never show my grief, my heartache.

Instead I built armor around my heart so no one would know, no one could see how losing you broke me. I have made a life without you. I am the alpha of alphas, the strongest of all Wyverns since the first sons. I am the Dragon Warrior all others fear. I do all of this your name.

A name I never thought I would say again. A name etched on my heart by the most painful time, a name I barely dared to think.

Until I saw you again for the first time in hundreds of years. Your name burned on my lips, the memories of you scorching my soul. A fire I thought long since dead, buried deep, sparked and ignited inside of me once again. Only when I called your name in the depths of Hell were you real to me.

Fallyn.

My Fallyn.

Damn you, Fallyn.

Why must you have such a stranglehold on my soul? Why do I need you so much it hurts? Why have you not been mine for all these dark years?

I will burn down the world to find you. Even if you and I are the only thing in existence not turned to ash, I would do it. To find you. To hold you. To show you my shattered wounded heart is yours and yours alone.

You may reject my offerings. You can slice my heart, my body, my soul with your blades, and still I will want and need only you. I have still never shed a tear, and my cold heart may never let me. But I have called out your name. When the night is the darkest and I wake having dreamt you were in my arms, your name slips from my mouth reaching no one's ears but my own with its mournful plea.

I am weak, nothing without you.

I cannot beg you to come to me, because you do not hear. I fear the only way we can be together is in Hell.

The final battle is coming. Good and evil will clash, and I

know you will be there. If it is the only time I have with you on this earth, I will take it. No other Dragon Warrior will battle more fiercely than I in hopes that by giving my all to defeat the forces of Hell, I can save you.

Even if you don't want to be saved.

That is my mission, my duty, my honor.

Then maybe you will be mine once again.

Until then.

Wieczni wierni,

--M

BE sure to read Match's book - the grand finale of the Dragons Love Curves series to find out what happens between Match and Fallyn.

WHO LOVES DRAGONS?

Dear reader,

I hope you loved reading these bite sized adventures and love letters in the Dragons Love Curves series!

The next book in the series is the grand finale of so be sure to follow me on Amazon, Bookbub, Facebook, to find out what happens next.

If you'd like to join in the fun of writing live with me, pop into my Facebook group Aidy's Amazeballs and join us every Tuesday for lots of fun and the first look at my brand new writing.

IF YOU HAVEN'T READ the book that started it all, check out *Chase Me* where you'll get to read about Jakob Zeleny, the Green Dragon Wyvern, and his mate Ciara's love adventure. You can binge read dragon shifters and their curvy mates for days!

Stay tuned to get your fix of sexy dragon shifters giving their mates happy ever afters (and happy endings! Lol)

I'd love if you left a review for this book. I really appreciate you telling other readers what you thought and how the book made you FEEL!

Even if you're not sure what to say – it can be as simple as

– "Read this in one sitting." or "Hooray for curvy girls and dragons." Just one sentence will do a lot.

Do you need more curvy girls getting their happy ever afters?

Want to be the first to know when the next book comes out (plus get cool exclusive content from me!)? Sign up for my Curvy Connection mailing list. Go here http://geni.us/CurvyConnection to sign up and I'll send you another curvy girl romance right away to say thanks for joining me!

You can always find me at www.AidyAward.com or in my exclusive reader group Aidy Award's Amazeballs on Facebook where we talk books, boys, and body positivity.

Kisses,

~Aidy

Surprise Me

Dirty Dragon

Crave Me

More dragons coming soon!

Alpha Wolves Want Curves

Dirty Wolf

Naughty Wolf

Kinky Wolf

ABOUT THE AUTHOR

Aidy Award is a curvy girl who kind of has a thing for stormtroopers. She's also the author of the popular Curvy Love series and the hot new Dragons Love Curves series. She writes curvy girl erotic romance, about real love, and dirty fun, with happy ever afters because every woman deserves great sex and even better romance, no matter her size, shape, or what the scale says.

Read the delicious tales of hot heroes and curvy heroines come to life under the covers and between the pages of Aidy's books. Then let her know because she really does want to hear from her readers.

Connect with Aidy on her website. www.AidyAward.com get her Curvy Connection, and join her Facebook Group - Aidy's Amazeballs.

Printed in Great Britain
by Amazon

40036320R00095